THE FIGURE
REVENGE

Ken Kirkberry

Self published

ISBN-13: 9798732469097

Cover design by: More Visual Ltd
Printed in the United Kingdom

"Thank you, the reader, for your continued support!"

Ken

CONTENTS

AN ARREST

Chapter 1

She awoke, her eyes were fuzzy and unfocused but, she made out the outline of the man on top of her. She watched as he lifted off her, he smiled, then stepped off the bed. She saw him throw on trousers, shirt, and shoes, before coming back to her at the bedside. Bending over, he gave her a quick kiss on the lips and said, "Thank you. See you again." With this, he left the room.

Her head was mixed up. She recalled eating dinner at a restaurant the night before and the cab ride home but after that...blankness. As she sat up the realisation of what had happened kicked in and she heaved all over the bed.

*****

New York was buzzing, a little known street just off Times Square was busy with Saturday night revellers.

A police car came to a screeching halt in the

middle of the street, sirens blaring; Officer Lowis sprang out of the car closely followed by Officer Dobbs, both broke into a stride before the car doors had even slammed shut, chasing after a fleeing man.

Officer Lowis shouted, "Police, freeze!" Drawing her nightstick with one hand, and her other hand covering her handcuffs. The man stopped and turned with his hands in the air. She walked over. The man smiled just as Lowis raised her handcuffs, then pounced forward, striking her on the chin. Lowis dropped to the floor. The man kicked her in the stomach, she immediately curled into the foetal position in an attempt at defending herself. Looking up, when the beating paused for a moment, she heard heavy footsteps. Officer Dobbs was nearly upon the man. The man turning away, started to run but Dobbs caught him quickly.

Dobbs screamed, "Freeze, you fuck!" as he raised his nightstick. He then hit the assailant on the back of the knee. The assailant dropped to the floor heavily, tried to turn and kick out but Dobbs swerved the kick and hit the assailant with the nightstick again, catching him in the face. Blood spurted from the assailants head as he finally lay still. Lowis had risen and caught up with her colleague. She snapped the cuffs on as Dobbs sat on the assailant. Dobbs advised the assailant of his rights, then addressed Lowis, "You ok, Laura?"

"Yeah, yeah, my jaw hurts like anything, but I'm ok!" Lowis gently manipulated her jaw. Then realising they weren't alone, she exclaimed, "Oh shit!"

Dobbs looked up frowning; there was quite a crowd gathering, most with mobile phones out. One onlooker shouted, "He's bleeding! Police brutality!"

Both officers stood, Dobbs pulling his prisoner up with him. Looking at the man's face, he realised his nightstick had caught the man on the side of the face and the gash across his eye and deformed looking nose were due to his actions.

"Let's get him to the car. The first aid kit's there," Dobbs instructed.

Lowis, through the pain, shouted, "Get back. Everyone get back, this man is under arrest!"

The crowd froze, then again the voice shouted, "Police brutality! You can't hit Dez like that. He's unarmed!"

Lowis placed her hand on her pistol and walked a step in front of Dobbs and the prisoner Dez, as they headed for the car. Lowis became more concerned as the crowd was getting bigger and the berating louder. Her heart lifted as she heard sirens. Three more police cars joined them. Officers climbed out of the cars with nightsticks drawn. The officers pushed back the crowd while Dobbs placed Dez in the car.

*****

Captain Mark Ward came out of the court, "A bloody shambles. It was fixed."

Forensic Detective Lisa Barrett addressed her captain, "Captain, please. Calm down or at least don't lose it here in the courthouse hall."

Ward gave his detective a discouraging look but, before he could reply Detective Sergeant Ray Freemond spoke, "Boss, come on, Lisa is right. Leave it for now." With this, Freemond grabbed Ward's arm and pulled him towards a side door. Barrett stopped, looked over her shoulder and saw Officer Dobbs being led out the front door with his lawyers by his side. She smiled at Dobbs, he responded with a sad smile and a shrug of his shoulders.

Freemond bundled Ward into the car. Once joined by Barrett he gunned the throttle and turned the car towards Murphy's bar. The journey was short and silent. Once inside the bar, Lisa ordered the drinks while Freemond and Ward found a booth and sat down.

"Hi, Lisa." Murphy, the bar owner, smiled as he welcomed Barrett.

"Six strong ones, please, Murph." Barrett returned the smile as she spoke.

Back at the table Ward continued as though he'd never left the courthouse. "Three months and the fucks find Dobbs guilty. Unbelievable!"

"Look, Captain, it was a setup. But the video evidence was the key that made it stick," Barrett announced as she returned with six shot glasses full of whiskey, placing them all in the centre of the table.

Ward thumped the table, "The video evidence! Yeah, it showed Dobbs hitting Dez, but missed the motherfucker hitting Officer Lowis."

Freemond spoke more calmly than he felt, "Captain, it's over now we can't do anything about it." Taking a breath, thankfully, Ward didn't respond.

Ward grabbed the first two shots, downing both; Freemond and Barrett did a shot each. Ward looked at his officers, rolled his eyes and reached for another, quickly downing that one too. He went to reach for the sixth, and last one, but not before Freemond slammed his hand over it. "What are you doing, Ray, that's mine?" Ward barked.

"Sorry, boss man, you've had three, so I thought I'd have one more," Ward smiled as Freemond downed the shot.

Barrett chuckled, "Captain, come on, let's slow it down a bit. Ray, three beers, please."

Freemond left them in silence and headed for the bar to get the beers. Barratt continued with a gentle tone. "Look, Captain, there's an appeal. I'm sure it'll get Dobbs off."

Ward glared at his detective before barking, "Was it me or you who had those whiskeys because those are the words of a drunkard!" Ward looked at the smiling Barrett and waited in silence for his beer. Accepting the beer from Freemond who had returned to the booth with Murphy by his side, he spoke again. "I'm ok. I'm ok, just disappointed. I read Dobbs and Lowis' report of the arrest, and the force was necessary. Dez hit Lowis, jeez he nearly broke her jaw!"

"Yes, Captain, but he did hit Dez hard, twice. The second one after Dez fell, that's what appears to be the issue," Barrett, flashed a smile to try and soften the message.

Ward knew Barrett and Freemond as friends, not just as colleagues in the precinct team, and most certainly not as inferiors, as their ranks implied to others. "Ok. Look, I'm going home before I drink this place dry." With this, Ward downed his pint in one and took off towards the exit.

Murphy, who had stayed standing next to the booth drinking his own beer, shouted at the leaving figure, "Hey! Boss man , stay, I could do with the sa...ouch!" Murphy stopped mid-sentence as Barrett's elbow hit him in the groin. Putting his hands up in surrender he went back to the bar.

Barrett turned on Freemond, "Ray. The captain is over wound up, don't you think?"

Freemond went quiet before answering, "Come on, Lisa. This is the fourth police brutality claim in the last year. Two good cops have been fired and two are awaiting their outcome..." He left the rest unspoken, knowing she'd understand what he was really saying.

"You think what they are saying in the precinct is true?"

Freemond thought before answering, "Yes. Since John did what he did two years ago the gangs are striking back."

Barrett let her mind go back to the events of two years ago. Her colleague John Mercer had murdered several gang members. One, Frith, a gangland lieutenant, Mercer killed in cold blood as revenge. Frith had killed Mercer's wife and daughter. "Yes. It's a kickback to John, but why not a gunfight, an all-out war?"

"The gangs are tough, but to take on the NYPD in a war would be fruitless. We'd bring in the army and all their weaponry, so it'd be suicide." Freemond paused and took a long swig of his beer.

"Picking away at us at every opportunity. Using the Press and modern media against us to darken our pride is the new weapon." Freemond thought again, remembering the video of Dobbs' attack on Dez was on the Internet within minutes of it happening.

"Look, Ray, I'm going to call it a night. See you in the morning." With this, Barrett hugged Freemond and left.

"Just you and me buddy," Murphy said as he joined Freemond to finish off the round.

*****

Unusually, Freemond was in before the captain. He sat at his desk with a large cup of disgusting coffee, although it was helping with his hangover.

"Morning, Captain," Freemond managed to croak as Ward finally came into the squad room.

"Morning, Ray. How long were you at Murphy's last night?"

"Too long, Captain. Wait, you seem quite chirpy?"

Ward smirked as he turned towards his office, he called over this shoulder, "Later."

Barrett had arrived and greeted Freemond, "Morning, Ray." Barrett sat at Mercer's old desk in front of Freemond's desk.

Freemond looked perplexed as he replied, "I'm getting too old for drinking but the captain...he must have had more at home, and yet he looks fine."

Barrett raised her eyebrows and took a look at the captain through his office window; he did look happy. "Did he say anyth...no wait!" Barrett exclaimed, "Today's the result of the mayoral election. Didn't the captain say his friend was favourite to be elected?"

Freemond paused before responding, "Yes, the result's being announced today. Dave Lacey, his old pal, is favourite. Do you think he might have it?"

Barrett didn't respond; both detectives looked up at the TV showing Fox news and stayed quiet, waiting for the news they knew their captain could really do with. Less than an hour had passed when the subscript flashed up on the screen, *"Dave Lacey is the new Mayor of New York."* The scream of "Yes!" from Ward's office confirmed their belief. Barrett stood and headed to the office, Freemond in tow.

"Your friend got it, Captain?" Barrett approached the desk as she entered the office.

Ward grinned, "Oh yes. Yes, he has. This is good news for us."

"Why's that, Captain?" Freemond sat in one of the tired armchairs across the desk from Ward.

Ward was beaming. "Dave, Mayor Dave Lacey now, was a cop here in New York. I trained with him; he was my first partner."

Barrett smiled, "So you said before, and...?"

Ward smiled, went to his hip and pulled out his hip flask. Ignoring the looks from his detectives, he raised the flask and took a long drink. Licking his lips, he said, "Dave will kick the gangs butts'. He's as straight as can be, takes no messing. Hell, he cleaned up LA; he was the DA there for years."

Freemond spoke, "Wow. Now you've said I do recall the name. He did one hell of a job in LA."

Barrett intervened and added, "I thought he was looking to get into politics, a senator, maybe?"

Ward gave Barrett a shocked look, shaking his head. "Barrett you should keep to talking to dead people. Being a mayor is politics!"

Barrett lowered her head as she went red. Freemond laughed at Barratt and added, "Captain, I thought he wanted LA?"

Ward sat at his desk, still smiling, "No. He's New York born and bred, he always wanted to get back here. Carnello and all the other motherfuckers won't continue to get away with shit like the

Dobbs caper anymore."

Barrett and Freemond both smiled at their superior, "Maybe things are finally about to change." Freemond's smile was as big as his boss'. "Hair of the dog, Captain?"

Ward gladly let Freemond take a swig of his hip flask. No more was said, and the day passed more positively than any one of the cops expected.

THE FALLOUT

Chapter 2

"Morning, Ray, you early again?"

Freemond acknowledged Sergeant Dean "Deano" Forest with a smile. "Hi, Deano. Yes, the pills are great, I sleep better, and I feel fine now." Deano, the desk sergeant, smiled back at Freemond. Grabbing a coffee, Freemond sat at his desk and noted the captains repeated absence.

Just after noon Barrett entered the squad room, "Hi, Ray. I hear you were in early again?" She asked whilst throwing a knowing look at Deano.

"Yeah, I'm good, thank you. Good sleep makes a huge difference." Freemond's straight back reply and broad grin looked suspicious to Barratt. He did look good for his fifty-odd-years, but she knew him too well to be fooled by his pretence.

"How about mentally?"

Freemond dropped his smile; only his wife and Barrett would get away with such a direct question. "Look, since my scare with cancer all is ok. Thankfully the pills and the op worked."

Barrett sat on the desk, "I know, but being desk-bound for almost four months since your return, must be sending you up the wall."

"'It's been nearly a year since I've been off the beat," Freemond responded.

"Haven't you thought of retiring?" Barrett asked.

"Come on, Lisa, you know I can't. My Toni has moved in with us and her husband Scott is working away a lot." Freemond looked up at his friend then realisation clicked like headlights being turned on full beam, "You've been talking to Gloria!" Barrett knew Freemond's wife Gloria well, they'd been friends for years.

Barrett jumped off the desk and headed for her lab, giggling on the way. Approaching the door, she stopped as the captain entered. "You smiling too, Lisa, something must be going on."

Barratt looked smugly at Ward, "Afternoon, Captain. You Ok?"

"Yes. Oh, wait, you have that new assistant downstairs, don't you?"

"Yes. Ged, why?"

"Good. Then you can go out for me."

Barrett looked a little taken aback, "Okay. Where?"

"Police business. You need to go and see Dobbs. See how he's getting on; I don't want the dickheads involved. It would be better for him if his colleagues went to see him instead."

"Colleagues, plural?" Barrett asked.

"Yes." Ward turned to address Freemond at the other side of the squad room. He shouted, "Hey, fatty. Move your butt and support Barrett!"

Freemond looked at his captain, smiled, grabbed his coat and joined Barrett.

*****

Nothing was said in the car. Barrett knew that although this was a health visit, Freemond was happy to be out and about. Barrett pulled the car up to the small detached house on a quiet street just on the city's outskirts. Both cops exited the vehicle and approached the man and child playing in the small front garden. "Hi, Dobbs. How are you, buddy?" Freemond smiled his welcome.

"Hi, Ray. Good to see you, and you too, Lisa." Dobbs hugged Barrett as they entered the garden.

"Wow, you're getting big young lady," Freemond addressed the child.

"Hi, Detective Freeman," the child smiled as she hugged Freemond.

Dobbs smiled, "Sorry, Ray, she always gets your name wrong."

"No problem. Is Anna in?"

"Yes."

"I'll take the little one in and say hello." With that, Freemond took the girl's hand and headed for the house.

Barrett had moved to the garden furniture and plonked herself down in a chair resting her elbows on the tabletop. "How you really doing?" Barrett asked Dobbs as he sat on the chair opposite.

"I'm fine so far. There's the appeal, so I'm distracting myself enjoying some time with Kirsty and Anna."

Barrett smiled, "The captain wanted you to know that until the outcome, he and the force will support you. That means full pay and everything."

"The captain's a good man, tell him thanks." As Dobbs finished the sentence, he caught a strange look from Barrett. "Come on, what is it, Lisa?"

"You believe the stories that this is all down to John?"

Dobbs stared at his clasped hands for a moment

then smiled. "You liked him. Were you an item?"

Barrett giggled fondly, "Not quite, nearly. It would have been good before he lost it. What he did puts a different stance on how I viewed him as you can imagine."

Dobbs giggled, "He liked you. We all knew. You were the only one that didn't know."

Barrett smirked, "Forget that and answer my question."

"Yes. We all believe this is Carnello and the other gangs getting back at us. Videoing my arrest is just a small part of it. I'm surprised they haven't got to the captain or Ray yet. Or you to be honest." Dobbs exclaimed.

Barrett shook as though someone had walked over her grave. "Ray has been off the streets for some time since his illness. The captain, well maybe he's best to be shown up by having his precinct constantly under threat?"

"Yes, possibly. Carnello can take his time. His warfare is different nowadays." Dobbs paused, "You know, even though I'm now involved in this, I don't blame John."

Barrett took a breath, "Come on, what John did was wrong."

Dobbs noted Freemond closing the front door

and making his way towards them, "Look, we may be in trouble at the moment, but no one in the precinct will blame John. The motherfuckers deserved what they got. Maybe it would be better if he was still around."

Barrett looked at Dobbs' gritted teeth. *And he meant every word of that,* she thought. Freemond broke the silence, "Great coffee, your wife makes. Talking of coffee while I'm out let's go and see Demis, Lisa, I need a bite to eat. I'll drive."

With Lisa in the passenger seat Freemond pulled into the road as she stared at the figure of Dobbs in the rear-view mirror.

*****

Entering Demis' bar both detectives were welcomed with a big hug from Demis, the owner. With a wide smile on his face, he said, "My friends it's great to see you. Ray, I thought you'd forgotten where my bar was!"

Ray chuckled, "No. I just needed good food instead of your unhealthy, grimy crap!"

"Hey, be nice. I have other customers!" Demis replied and laughed.

Barratt ordered a coffee for each of them after Demis made it clear the 'fancy stuff' Barratt requested wasn't available. Demis delivered the coffees and extras to the booth Freemond had chosen, "What you can have is a good ol' sausage bap on the house." Barrett and Freemond both smiled at this having heard their stomachs rumble on the way over there.

Having taken a few bites of the bap Freemond said, "Oh, I miss this: being out on the road; chasing the villains; catching a quick coffee and greasy food."

Barratt couldn't help shaking her head in exasperation before answering, "Maybe the too frequent trips to any and all available greasy spoons had something to do with the illness that almost killed you!" Barrett couldn't help being the medically trained forensic officer she was.

"So, I'll have what's left of your bap then?" Freemond challenged.

"No! Once in while it doesn't hurt." With that, Barrett put the remainder of the sausage bap in her mouth all at once, teasing her colleague.

Demis joined them with a coffee re-fill, "So, Demis, what's going on?"

"Come on, you guys, you know..." Demis looked around then spoke more quietly, "Carnello's fighting back...but I don't think he's at the root of it all."

Leaning forward in his seat, Freemond looked intrigued, "Really, if not him, who?"

Demis twitched in his seat and looked uncomfortable, "I'm not sure, but I hear things, can I tell you when I know for definite?"

Freemond frowned, this wasn't how Demi usually behaved, "Come on, tell us now?"

"No, no. I have to be sure. I'll add that a recent release of a Chicago prisoner may be of interest to you." With this Demis stood and quickly left them to it.

Barratt watched Demis walk to his kitchen, "He's spooked. Chicago?"

"Yes, and when Demis is spooked, there's trouble. You're the forensic let's see who has left Chicago lately."

"That's a detective's job!" Barrett laughed as she stood to leave.

"Yeah, but my eyes and those stupid computer things don't get on anymore," Freemond laughed while trying to convince Barratt all the way to the car.

*****

Upon their return to the station Barrett went straight to Freemond's computer and looked for recent Chicago prisoner releases. Within seconds her heart dropped...she knew one name...Frith.

"You look shocked, Lisa, who is it?" Freemond sat on his desk next to her.

"Tyson Frith was released six months ago."

"Oh, fuck!" Ray exclaimed, "Our Frith's big brother, I'd forgotten about him."

Freemond moved to sit at Mercer's old desk. "Tyson Frith is rumoured to be worse than his brother, possibly even a violent psychopath. We were onto him, but he moved to Chicago, so we lost track. I've heard stories about him and believe he was given five years for GBH. Although we know, or believe at any rate, he's a killer, that's all they could get him for."

"John killed his brother! Great!" Lisa thought out loud, "Any ties with Tyson and Carnello?"

"Yeah. Tyson was one of Carnello's, like his brother until he moved."

"Would Tyson have the influence here, now, to make it happen?"

Freemond thought, "Physically yes, the guy is a six and a half foot of muscle-bound freak. He boxed on the side and would have been a contender, but…"

"But what?"

"He has a temper and a short fuse, few would

square up to him face-to-face. Let's call it a day; I'll talk to the captain on my way home," Freemond said, looking at the empty captain's office.

AN UNWELCOME ARRIVAL

Chapter 3

As Captain Ward entered the bar, noting two detectives sitting at a booth, he headed towards Freemond and Barratt. Before he reached them, however, Demis blocked his way. "My God, the big man. Good morning, Captain, we are honoured."

"Hi, Demis, long time no see." Ward gave Demis a handshake then turned to join his officers. "Why here?"

"Morning, Captain, Ray's got used to being on the road again and can't do without eating dodgy food." Barrett pointed to the empty plate in front of Freemond.

"Come on, Ray, that's no good for you. Is Gloria not feeding you, hell, does she even know you come here to eat?" Ward challenged.

"Look who's talking!" Freemond responded

with a telling laugh, "And what drink, would you like, Captain?"

Barrett intervened, "Look, if the only two people in New York I love want to kill themselves with drink or a bad lifestyle then get on with it but stop bitching about it!"

Ward looked shocked, "We were only messing, Lisa. I didn't have a drink last night at all."

"I'm going to be both of your health coaches from now on!" Barrett's voice had risen and become stern. Freemond and Ward looked at each other warily.

"Can you give it about an hour as I need the business," Demis laughed as he provided four sausage baps and coffees as he joined them. "Rich man boss is paying, so I'll get some money from you guys at last." They all laughed.

Falling silent as they ate their baps Ward had a chance to think about how to broach the current problem with Demis, but decided to be direct, "So, why did you not tell us about Tyson Frith, Demis?"

Demis looked around wide eyed, "Quiet, boss man, you may not be scared of him but I sure am." Barrett, noticing Demis did look really scared, gave his hand a squeeze and smiled supportively at him.

"Look, the big guy is around and, yes, he has influence, so he could be behind this. Revenge for his brother would be probable." Demis advised.

"Probable?" Freemond asked.

"Yes, but he could only do it if Carnello supported him."

"Come on, Demis, what are you not telling us?" Ward pushed.

Demis looked up, "Sorry, boss man, I'm not sure yet, but there is something else happening. You'll need to leave it with me, and once I know, I'll talk. You scare me nearly as much as...the big guy," his voice had gotten quieter the more he spoke, his final words being almost a whisper.

Little more was said as the cops finished off their breakfast and left the bar. Outside, Ward turned to his detectives, "So, you're happy to be on the road again, Ray?"

"Yes, Captain. Lisa and I'll make some enquiries. I'll show her around."

Ward replied with a quizzical look, "I don't recall giving you permission to be back on the streets, let alone take my chief forensic as your partner?"

Barrett gave Ward a stern look before replying, "Hey, Ged is doing a great job at the lab and is very capable. I want to help my friend and having medical training, well, I can keep an eye on his health at the same time."

"Ok, ok, you win. Barrett, you're seconded to investigations for a couple of weeks with Ray as a refresh exercise. But if Ged messes up, I'll have your badge!" Ward finished with a wink before leaving his detectives.

*****

Freemond and Barrett spent the day visiting the parts of the city not generally seen by tourists. Barrett had been to many parts as a forensic but rarely chatted with the inhabitants. Around 4 pm on the Brooklyn Bridge Freemond said goodbye to a couple of youths he'd been speaking to. Heading up the steps with Barrett without saying a word he stopped some 50 yards along the bridge. Freemond looked out at the Island in thought. "It's a lovely city, my home, but boy are there some goods and some serious bads."

Barrett chuckled, "Yeah, I agree. Today was interesting. You know a lot of people, even if they're the wrong type."

Freemond chuckled, "Yeah, 30 years of being a cop does that to you."

"They all seem respectful towards you though?"

"Yeah, when I started, we'd clip them behind the

ear or just tell them off. Fair, but firm, as they say. Most were young'un's, virtually kids and didn't do any real harm. The gangs, although they were always there, used to keep to themselves. Now they encourage...no, they hide behind youngsters. Motherfuckers like Frith don't have to kill today, they just get some scared kid to do it for them. Drugs and money, drugs and money."

"Today proves Tyson Frith is back, but no one's gonna talk. That about sums it up?"

"He's one motherfucker that will kill without batting an eyelid. He scares the fuck out of me too."

Barrett looked at her colleague. He suddenly looked like the weary old cop he was. Barrett cuddled Freemond. "Come on, take me home and get Gloria to cook for me. There's not much better in life than that!" Freemond laughed knowing a good evening was in store.

*****

On the other side of town from Freemond's apartment, Officer Dobbs entered his local supermarket. "Good evening, Officer Dobbs," Patel, the storeowner, came around the counter.

"Hi, P, just Dobbs will do. You got any of those chocolate egg things with toys in?"

Patel replied, "Yes, round the back, for little

Kirsty…?"

Before Patel had finished, two men entered and stood behind Dobbs. Dobbs saw Patel's reaction and turned, hand on his holstered gun. "I'm a police officer, what's your problem?"

The first hooded man walked to the side of Dobbs and addressed Patel, "Go get that chocolate!" Patel left. The man addressed Dobbs, "No trouble, Mr Policeman, my boss just wants a word." He gestured to the bigger, hooded guy next to him.

Turning to the other bigger, hooded guy, "And you are?" Dobbs felt his skin crawl at being blindsided into being sandwiched between the two.

The figure smiled, perfect white teeth showing through a stubbly face. "You're not a cop anymore, or at least that's what the jury will confirm in a few weeks." Dobbs, unsettled, held his hand over his gun tighter. The hooded figure looked at Dobbs gun hand. "Come on, cop. If I wanted you dead, you would be dead already. Calm down; I just want a word."

Dobbs didn't release his gun hand, "And?"

The figure removed his hood, "Your colleagues have been nosing around asking about me. Well, you can tell them I'm here and not afraid of them or the NYPD. Tell them to bring it on. Tyson Frith hides from no one." With that, both men left.

Dobbs took a breath. Patel had returned to the front of the shop, "Are you ok, Officer Dobbs?"

"Yes, thank you, Mr P. I'll take the chocolate and this milk."

Patel smiled at Dobbs, "Look, have them on me. It's at times like this we need you guys in blue."

A MURDER

Chapter 4

"Morning, Ray, what are you doing in my lab?" Barrett welcomed her colleague.

"Good morning, Sergeant Freemond," Barrett's assistant Ged shouted from the other side of the laboratory.

"Hi, Ged." Then addressing Barratt Freemond looked concerned, "Dobbs called me early this morning."

"I know. He called me late last night. Ged, please go and get some coffees." Ged left the room.

"What! And you didn't call me?"

"No, you *need* your beauty sleep. Mine, well, it's natural," Barrett laughed.

Freemond laughed, "Look, Lisa, this is serious. Tyson Frith has threatened a cop, well actually he's threatened all of us."

"I know. Have you spoken to the captain?"

"No, he's out again."

"Then say good morning now."

Freemond turned to see his captain approaching them with another man beside him. The man looked younger than Ward, well shaven, wearing an expensive suit. Freemond knew the man from watching the announcement of the new mayor with Barratt, "Good morning, Captain. Mr Mayor, a good morning to you, too."

Dave Lacey smiled and gave Freemond a firm handshake. "Detective Sergeant Ray Freemond it's a pleasure to meet you." Barrett cleared her throat. Lacey turned his gaze in her direction, "Forensics Detective Lisa Barrett. Wardy has told me about you as well but didn't mention how beautiful you are."

Barrett blushed as she put her fingers through her long brunette toned hair. Ward quickly chastised him, "Come on, Dave, that's un-PC, you can't say things like that nowadays."

Lacey smiled at his friend, "I can if I say it to Freemond as well."

Freemond chuckled. Barratt laughed, and said, "This is a lab; I must have something to improve your eyesight, Mr Mayor."

All four laughed out loud. "So, what do we owe

the pleasure?" Freemond asked.

Lacey responded, "I've come to see Captain Ward and he thought it would be good for me to meet his team. Specifically, you two."

"Promotion?" Barrett flirted.

Freemond gave Barrett a disgusted look. "Apart from being the captain's friends, why else?"

Lacey walked around the room and then turned to Freemond. "Always the detective. I like him, Wardy. Look, we all know that this is to do with John Mercer and you three were heavily involved, so we need to be together on this."

"We're the NYPD, of course we're in this together, Mr Mayor," Barrett was trying too hard to impress.

Ward shook his head, "Cut the crap, guys. Dave is here to kick Carnello's butt."

Lacey laughed, "Such honesty, my friend, but yes, that's the plan. In this company only, it's Dave, please."

"Dave, then, you know Tyson Frith is involved?" Freemond stated.

"Yes, an interesting development. We kicked his butt when he was young. Wardy, you recall?"

"Yeah, but he was a kid then. He beat his teacher

for giving him an F if I recall. He's a man-mountain nowadays."

Lacey laughed, "Physical size is only good in a hand to hand fight. I, however, fight differently. Lisa, Ray, watch your backs, at some point they will come after you. Embarrassing us and causing my friend, Wardy's, precinct-problems seems to be their initial attack. Definitely a Carnello tactic for now which is harder to fight. Give me a few days to get back into the New York swing of things and then I'll help you. Wardy, your turn for lunch." With that, Lacey shook Barrett's and Freemond's hands again and left the laboratory, passing Ged on the way out.

Once the door had closed behind them Freemond taunted Barratt as he took a long awaited swig from the coffee Ged handed to him. "How old are you! He's old enough to be your father!"

Barrett went red, again, "Sorry, yes, I know, but he's so polished, in looks at least. But hey, if I were after an older man, I'd only have eyes for you, Ray."

"Bullshit, and you ate my wife's food the other night." Freemond chuckled, then added,

"Thanks, Ged, I'll take this upstairs, catch you later, Lisa."

*****

The day passed slowly, Barrett wished she was

outside, but Ged required further training and Freemond seemed to want to hug his desk again. Eventually, Barrett went to say good night but changed her mind, "It's Friday, Ray, a quick one at Murph's before home?"

"Yeah, I'll get my coat, shall we call it a date?" Freemond had not forgotten their earlier conversation.

Deano made a very dramatic show of picking up the phone, "Hello, Gloria, I have some bad news for you..."

"Stop it, you fool," Freemond's shout, was enough for Deano to stop his pretend call to Freemond's wife.

*****

Later, across town, Officer Townsend sat in her squad car parked beside a traffic light junction. As she studied the quiet street in front of her a dark coloured old Chevy car pulled up and stopped at the lights. Two women were inside; a dark-haired woman in the passenger seat looked at her, opened the car window and threw a bottle onto the sidewalk as the car pulled off. Townsend thought, *a little early for drunk driving but let's see.* Hitting the gas and the flashing lights, Townsend pulled the police car behind the Chevy The vehicle didn't stop straight away. Pulling into a car park behind an old deserted club, Townsend followed closely and pulled up behind. Fetching her torch and drawing her nightstick she approached the driver-side door. Tapping the car window with the nightstick, she called out,

"Open your window!" The blonde driver smiled but made no move to do as instructed. "Open your window!" Townsend shouted again, this time placing the nightstick on the car's roof and trying the locked door.

As the driver smiled once more, Townsend caught a glimpse of movement behind her in the window's reflection. As she turned the blow to her face laid her out cold.

*****

8am the next day, Barrett's cell rang. "No! No, not Townsend! She's my friend, please, no!" Barrett pleaded at her cell as she hit the throttle, siren blaring and lights flashing.

Freemond, on the other end of the call, replied, "Sorry Lisa, it is Townsend. Get here quickly but please, drive carefully."

Within minutes Barratt was on the scene. The run-down house on the south-side was on a virtually deserted estate. Exiting the car quickly, she ran into the house, stopping in her tracks at the sight of her friend's naked body laying on the floor. Freemond was the first to her side, "Lisa, don't do anything. You don't need to deal with this, I called

Ged, he'll be here in a minute or two."

Barrett shrugged past Freemond and stood above the body of her friend. With tears in her eyes, she shouted, "Bastards, we must get them!" Barrett then ran out of the house and sat on a wall.

A few minutes later Freemond came outside and hugged Barrett. "Ged will deal with this properly, you trained him well. Are you ok?"

"What happened?"

"Despatch hadn't heard from her for about a half-hour so called her around 9 pm without any response. Her squad car was picked up around 10 pm abandoned near the old Pink Club. They've been looking for her since then. Her mobile and gear were with the squad car." Freemond paused, "An anonymous call to the station around 7 am this morning pointed us here. I was called first."

"I had drinks with her the other night. Hell, she was going to get married. Dylan, OMG, what am I going to tell Dylan, her fiancé?"

"Leave it to me, I'll tell him."

"No, No! I will." With this, Barrett rose to leave.

"I'll take you." Turning to another officer, Freemond shouted, "Smithy, we're going to tell the next of kin. Get me all the details I need and fill me in later!"

Not even an hour later Barrett came out of the apartment building, opened the car door and sat next to Freemond. Freemond had been waiting, giving Barratt and Dylan time alone. It hadn't taken long, he'd only sat in the car alone for about five minutes. When the door clicked shut tears flooded down Barratt's cheeks. Freemond took her hand saying nothing, there was nothing to say. They didn't speak until they reached their destination, a cemetery. Without words, both exited the car and walked hand in hand towards three graves. They sat on a bench opposite the three headstones.

Freemond, although uncomfortable, said, "Look, this is the only place apart from home I can cry. Seeing you so upset hurts." Freemond couldn't hold back his tears any longer and allowed them to flow freely.

Barrett controlled herself, wiped her eyes and hugged her partner. "I come here to think. Everything is here, love, loss, friendship, laughter, pride and grief. John and his family were great friends."

Freemond looked at the three graves belonging to his partner, John Mercer, Mercer's wife, and their only child. "You know the estate where we found...I mean where we've just been, is where we found the Taylor girls body..."

Barrett looked up and thought, "Yes, it is. It's a heck of a coincidence. Tyson Frith can't be behind this, surely? He can't be bringing us back to John's crime scene just to hurt us?"

"Maybe, but it does seem too big a coincidence for my liking."

"Why don't they just take us on directly? I'd rather die fighting than seeing my friends suffer." Barrett looked perplexed, as if she knew the answer to her own question.

Freemond let it go silent between them for a while before adding, "Look, sitting here won't put the motherfucker behind bars. Let's go do our job."

Barrett smiled, "Let's."

AN ADMIRER

Chapter 5

On arrival at the station Barrett went straight to the laboratory. "Oh! Hi, Detective Barrett, I was just tidying up ready to leave...it's nearly 5 pm." Ged was looking hopeful as Barratt entered.

"Ok, any update on Towns...I mean the victim?" Barratt asked as she looked at the covered body on the nearest slab.

"No, sorry, nothing so far. Gloves and rubbers were used I'm sure," Ged informed.

Barratt took a deep breath and sat at a stool near the slab, "She was sexually assaulted?"

Ged took a second, "Yes, I'm so sorry, boss."

Barratt gave a brief smile, "Don't be, it's not your fault. I'll have a coffee then might take a look myself."

"You're the boss, boss. Oh, by the way, I had to move some things as I was working. I haven't finished putting everything away yet. The rape kit needs to go to the hospital for processing as well."

Barrett looked across to where Ged was pointing and scowled. "Hey, why have you gone through my things?"

"Sorry, boss, I was looking for more evidence bags, and well, those things were stuffed in a drawer in front of them."

Barrett went to respond but was stopped mid-thought as two men entered the lab; the first she knew. She caught his eye and scowled at his overly friendly welcome. "Hi, honey, how you doing today?" Frank Caine said as he approached Barrett, giving her a peck on the cheek.

Barrett replied awkwardly, "We finished some time ago, Caine. I'm not your honey."

Caine replied dismissively, "Oh, sure, well, maybe. Anyway, have you met Jeff?" He asked gesturing to the man next to him.

Barratt looked the man up and down; he was her age, very handsome and dressed immaculately in an expensive suit. "Hi, I'm Detective Lisa Barrett. Do I know you?"

Jeff smiled, and then shook Barrett's hand, "You met my father, Mayor Dave Lacey, yesterday. I'm Jeff Lacey, his son."

"Of course. You look so much like him...but younger," Barrett blushed as she said this.

Lacey laughed, "I hope so." Ged was hovering in the background. "And you are?"

Ged wiped his hands on his lab coat then shook Lacey's hand. "Mr Lacey, it's a pleasure to meet you. I'm Ged Croonan, Barratt's assistant."

"And you. So, Miss—or is it Mrs—Barrett? any update?" Lacey added, "I'm one of my father's aids so anything you tell me will be in confidence."

"It's Miss, however I'm not sure Mr. Caine thinks so. But in the lab it's Detective Barratt, if you don't mind. I'll keep the details within the NYPD for now until we know more, if that's ok."

Lacey made a mental note of Barrett's look towards Caine that was as sharp as her tone. "Detective Barrett, I've been with your captain most of the afternoon catching up on things, so I've been in the know up to now. I was so sorry to hear about your friend. Another sad loss to the city."

A tear came to Barrett's eye as she replied, "Thank you, Officer Townsend was a good, honest policewoman."

Lacey looked at the covered body on the slab, "Now is not a good time. We'll get the assholes that did this. Frank, let's get that meal. Detective

Barrett, I hope to meet you again."

Barrett smiled, "Yes, of course." As the two men left she shouted after them, "Oh! And it's Lisa!"

ABSCONDED

Chapter 6

"I hope you didn't sleep at John's desk all night, Lisa?" Freemond asked whilst putting a coffee on the desk next to Barratt.

"Morning, Ray. No, I worked late but couldn't sleep so came in early and...well, this felt like the best place to sit."

Freemond knew his friend was lying. "It's the only empty desk, no-one's taken John's place, or been my partner for that matter, in the last two years," Freemond chuckled as he said this.

"Hey, am I not your partner?"

"Ok, yes that's right, for two weeks. I'll say you're the best looking partner I've ever had," Freemond gave his best smile.

Barrett blushed, "So do something about it, stud!" Freemond froze for a second then spat out half his coffee as he, and Deano in the background, roared with laughter.

Freemond sat at his desk, "Seriously, Lisa, anything on the vic...I mean...Townsend?"

"Ged did a good job. I checked his results and there's nothing of use so far," Barrett dropped her head as she said this.

"We'll get the punk. You know that," Freemond tried to reassure her as best he could.

"I know we will."

"My office, both of you!" Ward ordered as he walked past their desks.

Entering the office Freemond closed the door behind them, "What's up, Captain?"

Ward could hardly control his anger as he spoke, "The stupid fool, he's run away. Idiot!"

"Who?" Barrett asked.

"Dobbs. He's gone. Taken his wife and daughter with him and disappeared."

"What! Captain, please be joking?" Barrett exclaimed.

"Has he left or is he missing?" Freemond asked.

"Missing, no, he's ok but he's has gone into hiding," Ward advised.

"When, how do you know?" Barrett questioned.

"Early this morning, I think." With this Ward looked up and around, then handed Barrett his cell phone.

Barrett read the text message then announced aloud. "Shit, he has. Ray, he says that Tyson, or at least he thinks it was Tyson, smashed his daughter's window while they were sleeping in the early hours of this morning. He thinks he'll never be found not guilty and needed to get away from it all."

"Fuck!" Freemond called, "Do we know where?"

Barrett rechecked the message, "No, he's just said he's gone someplace safe. Did you text him back, Captain?"

"Yes, but he's not replied."

"Then let's trace his cell," Barrett went to move but stopped as the captain spoke.

"Both of their cells are at his home, as is his car. We have uniform there as we speak." Ward had more of an idea as to what was going on. All froze as a knock was heard on the door, "Enter!" Ward shouted.

"What the fuck are you two dickheads doing here?" Freemond couldn't hide his displeasure as Internal Affairs Detectives Richard Jenks and Tom Head entered the office.

Jenks spoke first, "Hey, you can't say that, Free-mond!"

Ward stated, "He says what he wants in my office, Detective. Answer his question!"

Jenks looked at Ward, "Yes, Captain. We hear that Dobbs has done a runner and thought we would...help out."

"You assholes, you're just here to advise Car-nello!" Barrett had had enough already.

"Captain!" Head cried, "Some respect or I'll make an internal charge."

Ward thought, "Calm down, you two." Turning to address the two IA Detectives, "No, he hasn't run, what makes you think that?"

"You have a team at his house, criminal damage or something but he's not there." Jenks couldn't help but grin.

"No. Dobbs has taken his family to a safe-house under my orders until the appeal."

Head looked shocked, "Really, Captain, and you expect us to believe that?"

Ward walked up to Head and looked him in the eye, "Are you questioning my integrity, Detective Head?"

Head backed up before responding, "No, Sir...

I mean...Captain, but it's our job to know if he's run."

"Don't try me again, Detective." Ward stood tall.

Jenks intervened, "Of course, Captain, sorry. But if it were true, then IA should know. Can you tell me which safe house he's in, as I would like to see him. Check he's ok after the vandalism last night."

Ward turned and looked at Jenks, then smirked. "No, I won't. Dobbs is my officer, and I want him safe. Don't even think of claiming concern for him or his family."

Ward stopped as he caught Freemond walking towards them. "No, Ray, stop, it's time I said my bit." Ward turned and looked at the two IA Detectives. "We all know what trash you two are. Now get out of my office before I let my team investigate you both!" Jenks looked at Head and seemed to decide this was not the time to argue, both left with the eyes of every cop on them as they walked through the squad room to the exit.

"Way to go, Captain!" Barrett hugged Ward for good measure.

Ward smiled and then came to his senses. "What the fuck! Upsetting IA is not my best move. I had better go and see their superior. Meanwhile, you two keep this quiet, but it may be worth you going to Dobb's and see if you can pick anything up."

Barrett and Freemond needed no more encouragement and were out of the precinct in moments.

*****

Arriving at Dobbs' house Barrett asked her forensics colleague as they entered the house, "Hey, Tate, anything?"

"Hi, boss. No, just a broken window and nothing about what car it came from."

"Did they leave in a hurry?"

"Yeah, but it looks like bags and clothes from both bedrooms have gone plus toothpaste and other toiletries."

Freemond thought, *that makes sense, once you've decided a safe house is the only option you need those types of things.* He ignored Tate and the other officers.

"You guys want to look around?" Tate continued.

"Yes, give us ten minutes, please," Barrett ordered. With that, Tate and the other officers left the house.

"Why are you ignoring my team, Ray?" Barrett challenged.

"Come on, Lisa, I would trust most of them, but someone called the dickheads. The captain is buying Dobbs time, you know that."

"Yeah, ok. Let's have a quick look, see if there are any clues to where they've gone."

THE PRESIDENT

Chapter 7

Ten minutes later both cops left the building, signalling their colleagues in the garden to go back in. Barrett stopped Tate before she re-entered and whispered something in her ear. Neither Freemond nor Barratt spoke until they pulled up at Murphy's bar.

"It's a little early for a tipple, Ray." Barrett teased.

Freemond smirked and entered the bar, Barrett followed. Both ordered a beer and sat at a booth. "We need to get to Tyson, get him to chase us. Then blow his fucking head off," Freemond thought he had the solution, however illogical it might've been.

Barrett shook her head; "I wish it'd be as easy as that, but it's not."

"What did you say to Tate?"

"Nothing to give the game away, I ordered her

to tell the captain or me anything before anyone else. Tate is one of us good guys; we can trust her."

"Wow, look!" Was the unexpected response from Freemond. Barrett looked up to see Ward and both Lacey's entering the bar. Ward brought his guests to join Freemond and Barratt in their booth.

"Good afternoon, team, we've just had a long brainstorming session at the precinct and felt a beer or two is just what we needed to wind down." Ward stated as he sat.

Mayor Lacey sat next to Ward; Jeff Lacey gestured to the empty seat beside Barrett, "May I?"

Barrett beamed, "Of course."

Lacey senior spoke, "I've been here a few times before. Didn't we have one hell of a Paddy's night here once, Wardy?"

Ward laughed, "One hell of a Paddy's weekend if I recall!" Murphy, the bar owner, was just in time to join in the laughter as he delivered the beers. He walked back to the bar chortling to himself.

"Anything to go on, you guys?" Lacey junior asked.

"No, but we all know who's behind this. If he killed Townsend, he will pay for it." Freemond spoke out.

"Proof, Sergeant, we need proof." Lacey senior responded.

"We're working on that," Barrett joined in.

Lacey junior smiled, "Yes, and we're sure you'll find the evidence we need to get them."

Lacey senior smiled, looked around, then said, "Fuck the charade. Carnello and his type time is up. I have support coming in, but it'll have to be after the weekend."

Freemond looked shocked, "Now that's the type of language we need, how?"

Ward chuckled, "Get us some more beers you two, I want to talk to Ray and Dave alone."

Barrett and Lacey junior stood and walked to the bar. "Five beers, Murph."

"On their way!"

"Lisa, then?"

Barrett smiled and tossed her hair, "Maybe."

Lacey junior smiled, "My dad is great friends with your captain. Indeed the captain's my god-father."

"Really!" Barrett looked shocked.

"Yeah, they somehow bonded at the Police Academy, and they went out as rookies together.

Dad keeps telling me the story of Uncle Ward," Lacey laughed. "Well, that's what I called him when I was younger. Anyway, Uncle Ward saved my dad's life once. He dived in as some hood took a shot at him. Uncle Ward took the bullet in his arm, it left no permanent damage, thankfully."

"Wow. Who was the idiot who shot at them?"

"Carnello."

Barrett froze, "What, and he got away with it?"

"Yes. That's when it changed my dad's life. He soon realised the pen was mightier than the sword and took up politics. The rest, as they say, is history."

"Talking like he just did, does not sound very political?"

Lacey laughed, "Dad sometimes forgets, and his New York roots come back, especially around friends."

Murph put the beers on a tray next to them, "These are on the house. Thankfully New York's finest come here often, but the Mayor, wow...do you think he'll let me have a selfie?"

Lacey laughed, "Sure, go ask and take the beers for us, please." Murphy picked up the tray and headed for the booth.

"Quite the celebrity, your dad." Barrett teased.

Lacey looked at his father, "Yeah, he is. I know he's my dad, but...you just have to have respect for the man."

"Why do I feel a but is missing from that sentence?"

Lacey giggled, "No buts, he's a good man, just don't piss him off!" This took Barrett aback. "Sorry I didn't mean to swear, you'll get to know him. By the way, do you have a formal dress?"

Barrett looked perplexed, "Pardon, are you trying to chat me up?"

Lacey laughed, "Well, you'll need one for the meal on Friday evening at Sauce and Food. The President..."

"Wow, stop! Did you say THE President!"

"Yes. Didn't you know? No, of course, you wouldn't it's a secret meeting. Well until he turns up. You can't hide the President."

"A secret, why, what?" Barrett was confused.

"Barmy, as we call him, is here to celebrate Dad's election win. Just for a night, for a meal with a small group of friends."

"Barmy, you call *the* President, Barmy?"

"He calls dad, Lazy Lacey."

"Why?" Barrett looked surprised.

"Barmy is what, ten years his junior and yet he's made President and dad is still on his way. Of course, he got side-tracked with a police career and some military stuff."

"Your dad's planning on running for president?"

"Yes, and he'll win, in three years maybe. But all this is meant to be a secret. Anyway, you didn't answer my question. Do you have a formal dress?"

"Yes."

"Great, my chauffeur will pick you up around 7 pm. Oh, and don't tell anyone, please."

Lacey left the bar and joined the others in the booth; Barrett sat at the bar and watched them. "You ok, Lisa?" Murphy enquired from behind the bar.

"Yeah, Murph, yeah. I'm good," Barrett smiled.

A KID

Chapter 8

Barrett got into the car, "Morning, Ray, straight to the Zola house?"

"Morning, Lisa. Yeah, the on-site team have a few things on Officer Townsend's murder," Freeman replied as he manoeuvred the car through the New York traffic to the old estate on the south side. Where Townsend's body was found.

Both Detectives exited the car and approached a colleague outside the house. "Hi, Casey, what you got?"

"Hi, Barrett, see Stone inside." Freemond acknowledged Casey with a smile and led them into the run-down house. Detective Stone was standing next to a kid.

"Andrew Zola here has something to tell us." Stone looked at the kid.

But before the kid spoke, Barrett interjected, "Wait, kid. How old are you?"

He looked frightened, "I...I'm twelve, Miss."

Barrett smiled, "Are there any adults around here?"

"No. My brother was here a few nights ago when I was here, but I've been at a friend's and only came back today, all you guys were already here." The kid grew more nervous, fidgeting as he spoke.

Barrett gave Stone a disgusted look. "Andrew, I don't think your brother is about, so would you come to the police station with me, please? If you give me a number of your mother or another adult that you know and trust, we'll get them to meet us there."

As the kid thought about it Barrett gave him her most reassuring smile. "Ok, Miss. My mom died a few years back, but Aunty Lauren will help me."

"Thank you, Andrew. Give me the number and when we're in the car I'll call Aunty Lauren." With that, Barrett took the kid's hand and led him out.

As Freemond turned to follow Stone caught his arm, "Ray, what's she doing, he was going to tell me everything!"

Freemond shook his head, "Come on, Stone. A minor on his own with loads of cops and no adult? Any evidence would be inadmissible in court."

"Ray, I don't want evidence, I just need to know

where his shit big brother is so I can give him payback for Townsend."

"Just because this is Zola's house you assume he's the killer?" Freemond shook his head, "Let's do the job and do it the right way."

*****

An hour later they were back at the station; the kid was with his aunt in the main office. Barrett had done the pleasantries and was now at the coffee machine with Freemond. "Poor kid," Freemond started, "he's got no chance. His brother's a gang member and possibly a cop killer and I've arrested Aunty Lauren for drugs and prostitution a number of times. You shouldn't have called her. He won't say anything in front of her."

"I know, Ray, but it's the law. Anyway, here comes the cavalry." As Barratt finished, a Child Protection lawyer approached.

"Morning, Lisa, long time no see." Kayleigh Tapsul hugged her friend. "And Detective...no, Sergeant Freemond I recall?"

"Hi...Kay?" Freemond was unsure of her name.

"That will do. So, your job is to get auntie Lauren spooked about some old charges, scare her enough to let us interview him alone. You up for that?"

Freemond smirked, "Give me five minutes. " With that, he went to the office where the kid and Lauren were sitting. He spoke into Lauren's ear, after a short discussion she got up and followed Freemond to an internal office. Freemond shouted, "All yours. You have her permission," before he closed the door behind them.

Barrett and Tapsul entered the office, Barrett spoke, "Hey, Andrew. This is Kayleigh Tapsul. She's a Child Protection lawyer, so she's here to help you."

Tapsul smiled and sat down next to the kid, "That's right, Andrew. If Detective Barrett asks you questions you cannot answer or don't want to answer then let me know and I'll help you."

"Are you her boss?"

Tapsul laughed, "No, but I can keep her in line."

Barrett smiled, "So, Andrew, have you been living with your brother for some time?"

"Yes, since Mom died."

"I'm sorry to hear that. Is your father around?"

"No, you guys have him. He's in jail for killing Mom." The kid lowered his head and subtly wiped a tear from his cheek.

Barrett sat upright with shock. "Oh, I see. I'm

sorry. It must hurt when you speak about it?"

The kid thought, "Yeah it did before, but Aegeus took me. He taught me to be tough, and if anyone at school teased me, I'm to split their lip." With that the kid hit out with a punch to emphasise his point.

Barrett moved back, the punch was not meant for her but was too close for comfort. "Wow. Well, you don't need to do that here. We only have sympathy for your loss." Barratt smiled reassuringly and the kid smiled back. "So, when did you last see your brother?"

"As I told the cop at the house, Aegeus said he needed to do something at the house, and I had to go to my friend's. I do this most Friday and Saturday nights as Aegeus likes to party, but he's not normally gone for this long."

"So Ageues told you to stay longer?"

"Yeah, he called me on Sunday and told me I had to make do for a few days, and he'd call when he could. He said, not to go home as you lot were there. But I fell out with my friend this morning on the way to school and had nowhere to go but home."

Barratt's heart ached for the poor kid, "I'm sorry to hear that Andrew. Couldn't you have gone to Aunty Lauren's?"

"No! I don't like it there. Her boyfriend's beat me up or make me run chores for them like nicking booze."

Barrett looked at Tapsul who gave a reassuring nod. Barrett continued, "Look, Andrew, Kayleigh can find somewhere clean and safe with good food for you, and you can stay there for a few days. Is that ok?"

"Yeah. Couldn't you protect me? I mean being a cop?" The kid went red as he said this.

Barrett smiled, "No. I'm sorry, Andrew, but I have to protect the city. Besides I'm a crap cook." The kid and Barrett chuckled together. "I'm sure wherever Kayleigh takes you I can visit, though."

"Yes, of course, Detective Barrett." Tapsul reassured.

"So, before you go, young man, do you know where your brother is?"

The kid appeared to think hard before saying, "No, he didn't say, but he was on Helen's mobile when he called."

"Oh wow, and Helen is?"

"His girlfriend. She's ok but not as pretty as you, Miss." Again, the kid went red.

Barrett gave her best smile, "Thank you. Can I

have Helen's number or her address, please?"

The kid pulled out his cell, looked up some numbers and said, "Here it is. I don't think she has a house as she lives with us."

Barrett took the cell and wrote down the number, "Thank you again, Andrew. You'll need to go with Kayleigh now. I'll tell Aunty Lauren." With that they all stood with Tapsul motioning the kid to the door. As they got near to it Barrett asked, "Hey! Sorry Andrew, does Helen have a surname?"

"Helen Georgio," the kid replied and waved to Barrett as he exited.

Barratt crossed the office to Mercer's old desk and plonked herself in the chair. Freemond sat on the corner of the desk. "Bet the kid was putty in your hands!"

"You know, I actually feel really sorry for him."

"So, do we get anything?"

"Aegeus Zola called his little brother on Sunday from Helen Georgio's mobile, who appears to be his girlfriend. The IT bods are finding its location together with Georgio's address as we speak."

"Wow, we could make a Detective of you yet!" Freemond attempted a compliment.

Ten minutes later the Mercer's desk phone rang, Barrett answered it. "Ok, yes, give me both addresses again... Great!" Barrett picked up the post-it she'd written the addresses down on and jumped up, "Let's go!" As they passed Deano, Barrett requested an unmarked car to watch one address until they got there. "They're watching for Aegeus Zola or Helen Georgio. Both have records and have pictures on file. And have two squad cars follow us downtown to the other address." Deano nodded and started making the calls.

THE SEARCH

Chapter 9

Freemond pulled the car up at the first location, a building site on the south side with the Statue of Liberty in full view across the river. "You really think we'll find Zola or even his cell phone here?" Freemond asked as he exited the car.

"Unless he's a builder then probably not. My guess is the cell has been dumped. It was the last place it pinged on Sunday evening." Barrett looked around hopeful it wouldn't be a wasted search.

"Hey! You can't park there! Move yourselves, there's heavy machinery round here!" A man in a bright yellow bib shouted.

Freemond walked up to the man. "Sorry, buddy, but I can." Freemond flashed his badge, "You're going to have to stop work." Just as he spoke the two squad cars arrived.

"Fuck, I'm going to have to call the boss." After a short phone call, he started shouting to the workman close by, "Everyone stop but don't leave. Meet at the fire point." The two uniforms joined him in directing the workers.

"We'll need more men if we're going to search here," Barrett stated.

"Hey, you're with the forensic team, get your guys in." Freemond wanted to slip the search.

"I'll get the team in, but you aren't getting out of the search." Barrett turned with her phone in hand.

Freemond stood still, "I'd go for the skips first if I were you." He shouted with a chuckle, but his laughter was short-lived.

"Detective, why have you shut down my site?"

Freemond turned to see his accuser. "Well, Mr Caine. Fancy seeing you here?"

Caine froze, "What? I'm sorry, Detective, this is my site, so I need to be here. I repeat, why have you stopped my men working?"

Freemond chuckled, 'Your ex is calling in the cavalry, ask her."

Barrett had turned and heard this. "Asshole!" Turning to face Caine, Barratt's face was a picture of professionalism. "Mr Caine. We have reason to believe that a suspect or at least his belongings are on site and we need to conduct a formal search."

"Mr now is it?" Caine frowned, "I hope you're not using that badge to harass me."

Barrett walked closer to Caine, "If I were to harass you, then you'd know it!"

Freemond had seen enough, "Now, now!" he said as he split them up. "Detective Barrett go and start the search. Mr Caine, I'm sure, being the stand-up citizen you are, you understand the pressures the police force are under and want to do all you can to help our investigations." Getting very close to Caine's ear Freemond whispered, "Fuck with my friend, and you won't need a career."

Within the hour there were twenty or so Police officers on the site. Having checked the thirty-odd workers' identities, Zola not being one of them, the bins and site's search started. Leaving her team to search, Barrett found a coffee van and purchased coffee's for both her and Freemond. She was stood at the riverside looking at the statue in the distance.

"So, it's true you and Caine have split up?"

"Come on, Ray. I told you that months ago. It was a mistake from the start. We got close after his sister was killed. Ironic really when my supposed boyfriend had killed her."

Freemond took his cup and a swig of the coffee. "You know since then Caine has helped us with

Carnello amongst other things, and yet we still have nothing concrete on him. Pardon the pun."

Barrett smirked, "Yeah, that's my feeling, but the captain thinks this is a cat and mouse game and Caine is more likely to get Carnello on taxes than we are on gangland murders."

Freemond thought, "The Capone theory. You're probably right, but I still get the feeling Caines playing us."

"Me too. That's one of the reasons we split, not that we were together, it was just a couple of dates in all. Anyhow, you don't like him for other reasons, do you?"

Freemond took another swig of coffee. "When my Toni's husband, Scott, had an issue on one of Caine's sites, well Carnello's, not only was he fired but I think they put the word out so Scott couldn't get any more work. That's why he, Toni and lovely Charlotte moved in with us. He's working now but out of town, so he stays away a lot."

"It would be the kind of thing Carnello would do. Caine, though, I'm not so sure? Or is he just carrying out orders?"

"Who knows. The land of the free!" Freemond raised his cup to the statue.

Barrett's cell rang, "Hi, Vids, what you got?" Having listened Barrett started to cross the road,

Freemond followed. "Traffic camera..." Barrett stopped, looked at a photo that came through on her messages, and looked up at a road sign behind her, "caught a car stopping here late Sunday. Someone got out and threw something over the fence." Zooming in on the photo Barratt saw something of use. "Looks like a health and safety helmet sign." Barrett scanned the site boarding in front of her. "There! That sign. Let's see what's behind it."

Within a few seconds, Barrett had entered the works' site gate and was looking to her right. "Tate, over here! The big, uncovered blue skip in the corner, concentrate on that one!"

"Thank God, you stopped, Lisa. I've not moved like that for some time!" Freemond said gasping for breath.

"Sorry, Ray. Are you ok?"

"Yeah. Did Vids say who threw whatever it was over the fence?"

"No, the quality's poor but...the plate shows it was Helen Georgio's car."

"Nice. I'll call Casey, he and Stone are watching her apartment."

Within half an hour the goods were found as one officer climbed from the skip, "One mobile and one gun, boss!"

"Bag it and get it to my lab. Look around a bit more just in case there's anything else but I think that's all we're after. We're off!" Barrett ordered as she signalled Freemond to the car.

*****

Barrett pulled up behind Stone's car. Getting out they took the short walk and got into the back of Stone's car. "Hi, guys, any movement?"

"Hi, Ray. No. Not even for coffee."

"I'll go," Casey said reluctantly before exiting the car.

"What about the rear, if you guys have been sitting here without watching the back I'm gonna lose it?" Barrett asked.

"We checked that when we arrived. No proper rear, just a fire escape, which comes out in the alley over there," Stone pointed to a narrow alley at the side of the house, "which we can easily see from here. Is this going to be an all-nighter, do you think?"

"Not sure, but Deano has put a shift together just in case. What do you think, Ray?"

"Unlikely they'd be there. It'd be too easy. Besides, why call the kid knowing they could be traced then hide the cell and gun only to sit at his girl's place?"

"Assuming the cell and gun is Zola's, then that would be right. Let's have coffee and think." Barrett had noted Casey was coming out of a café with four cups.

*****

Back at Ward's office Lacey was meeting with Ward. "Are you sure, Dave?"

"Do you have anything but alcohol in this office, Wardy?" Lacey replied.

"I'll get Deano to get you a coffee."

"Water please, just water. I can't drink coffee like we used too. And neither should you, pal."

"Come on, it's my one vice. Anyway, meeting Carnello directly...that would be...interesting."

Lacey smiled, "Come on, Wardy, you know us public people have big egos and love a game. Even though he's on the wrong side Carnello is no different a beast."

Ward laughed, "So finally you show your true colours, a beast are you?"

Lacey laughed, "My political and business side say guilty. You know you should've come to LA with me."

Ward thought, "Yeah, it was a great offer. But for all my pains this is my home, this is my job. I love

New York, as they say."

"Then let's make it great again. I'll get Jeff to arrange the meeting... Oh, by the way, the Barrett girl, what's she really like?"

"Why?" Ward challenged.

"Suspicious of your old pal, Wardy?"

"No, just wanted to know if that's a professional or personal question?"

"Both. Jeff seems to have been enchanted with her already and, well, I normally vet his women."

"I'll take that as you being an overprotective father then," Ward chuckled. "Lisa is like a daughter to me. I've known her for years. Extremely professional and one of the nicest, warmest people I've ever met."

"No boyfriends, or baggage?"

"No, not really, just the usual, fell in love quite young and married an idiot barrister, James... whatever. Anyway, that failed and now she's at the latter end of her twenties...no, she was 30 last year...she's focussed on her career as far as I know."

"And this Caine guy?"

"You don't miss much. No, definitely not now; although they may have dated a few times."

"He's your Carnello snitch?"

"Yes. He swore to revenge his sister's tragic death and has been providing evidence and updates on Carnello. Mainly business stuff so we hope to get him on fraud at least."

"You don't seem so sure?" Lacey pushed.

"It's slow. I'd prefer it if he could tell us where a smoking gun is as such, and we could just go bust Carnello. But as I'm sure you know all too well, Carnello doesn't touch the dodgy stuff anymore; he just hangs it on a minion."

Lacey chuckled, "And the Mercer guy? A terrible story but he sounds like a real honest man who just got pissed off."

"Pissed off! Yeah, that would cover it. Seriously though, John was a great cop until the terrible murder of his wife and child. Was he wrong? Maybe. Do I blame him? No."

Lacey gave him a reassuring pat on the shoulder. "Look, buddy, I'm more inclined to go with Mercer and his ways, I just hide it better. We'll get Carnello, in the end." With that, Lacey headed for the office door.

Ward called out before the door was opened, "Jeff! If he's serious, he'd be a good match for Lisa. I love them both so no games, Dave. And I'll be happy to tell Jeff that Lisa is not to be just one of his conquests."

Lacey laughed, "You know, Jeff is more scared of his godfather than me. I think he's grown up, so yeah, if it goes somewhere, let's support them both."

*****

"Ray, you're snoring!" Barratt said as she shook her partner.

Freemond moved uncomfortably in the passenger seat before addressing his partner. "Fuck! It was your choice to relieve Casey and Stone. What time is it?"

"1 am Ray. And I've been watching all evening."

"Let me get some breakfast or something," Freemond had not fully awakened.

"Don't bother, cover's just arrived. I'll drive you home."

A GREEK CONNECTION

Chapter 10

"Ray, are you ill? You look like shit!"

Freemond looked up from his desk. "Morning, Captain. A late reconnaissance last night. Actually, I should have time off in lieu rather than being at this place for 9 am."

"You got here at half nine and have been sleeping for the last hour, Ray!"

Freemond looked towards Deano. "How can I legally kill a colleague, Captain?" Deano caught the comment and headed for the coffee machine, soon delivering Freemond a coffee as a make it up gift.

Twenty minutes later, Barrett entered the squad room and sat at Mercer's desk. As she turned to Freemond she opened her mouth to speak but he beat her to it. "Go away. How the fuck do you look so good when I feel like death warmed up?"

Freemond scowled, holding his coffee in one hand while holding his head with his other hand.

"Wow, Ray, you got out of bed on the wrong side." Barratt looked towards the others in the room and smirked, "Or was sleeping with me that bad?"

Freemond went to throw a cutting come back at Barratt but saw Deano and other officers pretending to sleep and snore. "You bitch, you told them. Our friendship is over." Freemond rose and headed for the john, laughing all the way.

Barrett entered the captain's office. Ward smirked, and said, "I'm putting you up for an award. Outstanding commitment to duty for dealing with Ray's snoring."

Barrett giggled, "Hey, be serious. This has been the first week that Ray's been on the road and I'm concerned about him."

"I know." Ward was more optimistic than Barratt felt. "His medical results, considering what he went through, are great. To be honest, he's as fit as a middle-aged man should be. Maybe he's just tired; as you say he's not been out and about for some time so it might be a bit much for him. You'll keep an eye on him for me?"

"Does that mean I can continue to be his partner for a while?"

"Yes, as long as Ged keeps progressing. Although, I'd prefer you off the streets and hidden in the lab."

"Oh, Godfather Ward, you're so nice." Barrett mocked.

"On another note, you know Jeff's a good guy."

"Jeff Lacey? Are you playing matchmaker now?" Barrett teased.

"No! I'm not playing games, Lisa. You're old enough to make your own decisions."

Freemond slouched into the office behind Barratt. "Nice for you to join us, Ray. So, how's the investigation going?"

"The cell and gun have Zola's prints all over them." Barrett lost her smile, "And the gun matched one of the bullets in Townsend."

"One of the bullets?"

Barrett turned and looked out of the window. "Five shots killed her. All five are from different guns. The assholes used her as target practice after…"

"I get the picture," Ward interrupted. "So, Zola is one of our main suspects. We already have an APB out on him. Maybe some close-quarter discussions would pull something up?"

Freemond responded, "Ok, boss. Lisa, I know a few people who may talk. And, of course, Helen Georgio's father is a friend of Demis so he might be good to talk to as well."

"Demis first. But no breakfast!" Barrett ordered as they left the office.

*****

"Demetrius Georgio, now he's a good man. All us Greek decedents are," Demis smiled as he said this, adding, "Demetrius is such a good name for a guy!"

Freemond and Barratt had arrived at Demis and ordered a coffee to go.

"We don't want a history lesson just information on where we can find him, and if he'll help us." Barrett was straight to the point with Demis.

"Who rattled your cage this morning, Detective Barrett. No manners and no breakfast? I'll go out of business!" Demis said indignantly.

Freemond looked at Demis, "Zola is Helen Georgio's boyfriend. We believe he was one of those that murdered Officer Townsend."

Demis froze, "Sorry. Give me five minutes." Demis did as he said and returned five minutes later. "Demetrius will meet you here at 3 pm."

Barrett smiled, "Thank you. Do you know anything yet? I want this fuck and those that helped him!"

Demis looked into Barrett's eyes; he'd never seen her like this before. "I'm sorry, Lisa, but all's gone quiet. Tyson's involved I'm sure of it, but I can't prove anything as yet. You'll be the first to know when I have something." Demis suddenly looked more hopeful, "Look, Darius is one of Zola's best buddies, you know him Ray. You'll find him on the outside basketball courts near St Mary's mission. It's worth a trip."

*****

Fifteen minutes later Freemond pulled the car up next to the basketball courts. "You know this, Darius?" Barrett asked.

"Yes, that's him!" Freemond was pointing to a dark-skinned young man with chiselled cheek bones, a strong jaw and defined muscles.

Lisa was taken aback, "Wow! He's a good-looking young man. How do you tan like that in New York!" Freemond shook his head in disbelief and exited the car, Barrett followed.

As they entered the court, the game stopped and one lad shouted, "Ah, come on, Detective Freemond, leave us alone. However, your girl can referee, she ain't bad for a cop." The group of young lads fell about laughing.

"Donaldson is it?" Freemond shouted. "Haven't we still got your car in the compound for non-payment of parking fines?" All the other lads turned on Donaldson and mocked him.

"Ah, fuck, man." Turning back to the group of youths Donaldson gestured to the side-lines. "Drinks break, guys." Once standing with Barratt and Freemond, Donaldson was more polite. "Surely you're not arresting me for some parking fines?" Donaldson placed his hands together as if to pray, mocking Freemond.

"No. It's Darius we wish to talk to," Barrett advised.

All the lads mocked again as they turned to a member of the group. The destination of their gazes went red but smiled, "I'll talk to the pussy but not you, Freemond."

His friends all exclaimed at that, some looking a little wary at his challenging use of language. Barratt smiled and approached Darius as he came forward, Donaldson made his way back to the group and helped himself to a coke. "This pussy bites. You sure you want to try me?"

All the lads laughed and backed off to the other side of the court. One shouted, "You're busted, Dari!"

"I'm Detective Barrett and I have some questions for you." Barrett was face-to-face with Darius. "Your friend, Aegeus Zola, we need to find him."

Freemond caught the look in Darius's eyes, "Don't run, Darius. I'm too old to chase you so will be forced to shoot your skinny butt before you even get to the fence."

"Mr Freemond, I won't run, but I don't know where Zola is."

"Your reaction suggests differently?" Barrett pushed.

"Look, we're all good guys, but Zola's in with the wrong people. They are bad people, and we want to keep out of their way."

"I know that, Darius," Freemond said. "How's your father's shop doing?"

Darius smiled, "The shop's doing ok. Not great but it keeps a roof over our heads."

"Look, I might pop over there at the weekend and say hello. I need some home improvement bits. He sells kitchen cabinet hinges?"

"Yeah, I think so. Zola's gone into hiding...I don't know why but he isn't talking to anyone."

"Including his best buddy?" Barrett pushed again.

"It'll not come from me, but if I hear I'll let you know. I don't think the gang he's in will look after him anymore."

"Thank you, Darius," with that Freemond patted the boy on the back.

Freemond and Barrett left the court hearing "Did you get the cop-chick's number?" followed by lots of laughter.

Before Barrett could say anything, Freemond spoke, "Hey, wait. That's Reynolds!"

Barrett wasn't quick enough before Freemond walked up to the man. "Private Reynolds, right? Man, you look good!"

The man turned around with a broad smile and said, "Detective Freemond, great to see you again."

"Ahem." Barratt came up behind Freemond and tapped him on the shoulder.

"Oh, this is my new partner, Detective Barrett. Lisa, this is Private Reynolds. We, John Mercer and I, I mean, met him a few years back while investigating...a murder."

Reynolds shook Barrett's hand, "Any partner of Detective Freemond or Mercer is a friend of mine."

"You knew John?"

"Yes. Detective Mercer interviewed me about

the shooting of two hoodlums at the lights near the Birdcage. He got me back into the mission, since then I've cleaned up and gotten a job. I'm taking these cookies into the mission to say thank you, as I do every week I might add."

"That's great, Reynolds. It's good to see," Freemond said warmly.

"Of course, we didn't know then who the murderer was, and, to be honest, I still can't believe it. I owe my life to Detective Mercer even if others don't." Barrett looked a bit uncomfortable. Reynolds picked up on it, "Hey. I'm not worshipping Mercer, although many around here see him as a hero. If it weren't for the gang culture more people would have a chance in this city." Thinking he would lighten the conversation Reynolds turned tactics, and addressed Freemond, "Do you remember the night you turned up at the mission with that butt of a detective, he was a Vietcong sympathiser, right?"

Freemond howled with laughter. Once he'd regained control of himself he turned to the puzzled Barratt and explained. "Head and I went to the mission afterwards to further interview Private Reynolds. But I kind of told Reynolds that Head was a Vietcong sympathiser. Boy did Reynolds give him some stick. It was hilarious."

Barrett laughed. "Hey man, it's really good to see you doing well. Here's my card, keep in touch."

With a handshake the cops left.

*****

3 pm was upon them soon enough, Barrett and Freemond had arrived back at Demis' bar and were sitting at a booth with a couple of coffees as an old Greek man sat opposite them. "Mr Georgio, thank you for coming," Freemond respectfully rose from his seat as the elderly man sat down. Taking the man's hand Freemond shook it gently.

"This is Detective Barrett. You want some coffee?"

Georgio smiled, "No, Demis is a good friend, but I wouldn't drink his coffee, I've lived too long to risk it." All three laughed before Georgio continued with a matter of fact tone, "You're after my Helen?"

"Yes. Although it's her boyfriend, Aegeus Zola, we want to speak to." Freemond replied.

"That asshole...is she in trouble with you guys?"

Barrett joined in, "No. We don't believe so, but she could have some information we need."

"And that information is for the investigation into the murder of a police officer?"

Freemond answered, "Yes, Mr Georgio. It sounds like you know something."

"There are rumours. How my little girl got caught up with a shit like this I don't know. At the moment Helen is missing; I've not seen her since last Friday. My wife is distraught. If you find my daughter, will you protect her?"

"Our job is to protect, Mr Georgio," Barrett advised.

"Unless of course she's involved and then you guys will stick together. You are but a gang with a badge?" Georgio challenged.

Barrett didn't like this, Freemond, sensing her discomfort, put his hand on her thigh below the table. Freemond addressed Georgio, "Look, Mr Georgio. In some ways I can see where you are coming from but, we are the law, and our intentions are good. I'd say Helen mixed up with a gang is far more dangerous than her being of interest to us, wouldn't you agree?"

Georgio thought, "If she calls me and I can help you find Zola and her information is of use to the investigation you won't need to charge her. Can we have a deal?"

Freemond pushed harder on Barrett's thigh. "We'd do our best to reduce whatever charges were filed against her if she does end up being involved, of course. Do you know where they are?"

"Sadly, no. Helen will call me. Once she does I'll

let you know. I'm putting the life of my daughter in your hands, Detective Freemond."

"I'll do what I can, Mr Georgio. Finding Helen and getting her away from Zola has to be my first priority."

Georgio rose, "I'll see what I can do. Good day to you both."

Once Georgio left the bar Barrett spoke up, "His daughter could have been involved in my friends' murder, and you want to do a deal!"

"She's probably a victim too, Lisa. Calm down, we'll get the information we need. And we need Zola, right?"

"And a wee shot!" Demis had joined them with three whiskies. Freemond and Barratt gratefully accepted the shots and downed them immediately.

Barrett turned to Demis, "Thank you for organising for Mr Georgio to meet with us, he may be of some help. Demis, I know you know something. I can feel it every time you come near me. I'm waiting."

Demis looked into Barrett's eyes, "Hell, I thought Ray and John were scary but you, you're something else!"

Barrett persisted with a lower tone to her

voice, "Tell us!"

Demis moved uncomfortably in his chair. "Tyson led the killing of Townsend, and there are more planned. Maybe you cops should double up for the time being."

"Give us firm evidence and we can get him off the streets for good.!" Barrett had no patience left.

"Wow, Lisa. Demis is our friend so calm it!" Freemond turned on his partner.

"No, Ray, leave her. I can understand her frustration. Lisa, if and when I have something that'll stick, I'll let you know. But these guys are good. If they use a weapon, it'll be gone. If it's gonna be messy then they bully a minion into doing it. Tyson and Carnello would be clean even if you raided them."

"Fuck!" Barratt thumped the table.

"Demis, this is getting out of hand, we need to stop it." Freemond interjected.

"If Zola was given to you on a plate, would that help?"

"It's a start."

"Leave it with me, Ray. I can get the word to someone who may be able to help."

"Wait!" Barrett couldn't hold her tongue. "More

deals... No, I want Zola and the other four fucks that did this. And maybe Carnello as well!"

"Time to leave now, Lisa," Freemond was firm.

THE MEETING

Chapter 11

"Good evening. Wow, you look different outside of your normal jeans and blouse!"

Barrett smiled at Jeff Lacey as she stood to accept his peck on the cheek. "Thank you, Mr Lacey. I do have legs, you know."

Lacey looked down at Barrett's uncovered legs. "And nice ones at that!" Both sat at the booth.

Murph was on his new customer quickly, "What will it be, Mr Lacey?"

"Any gin, but with a kick please," Lacey replied.

"Another for you, Lisa?"

Barrett went red, "Yes, please."

Murphy moved off to get the drinks. "I saw your gin glass, so I thought I'd give it a go. So, is tonight work or leisure?"

Barrett giggled, "Let's hope it's not work, after a

couple of these, I'll be no good to anyone."

Lacey thought, "Interesting...but it looks as though work comes first." Barrett followed Lacey's eyes and noted Lacey senior and Captain Ward had entered the bar. All four smiled, acknowledging each other. Ward and Lacey senior sat at a booth near the back, cordoned off as a private area.

"Well, police protection has never looked so good," Lacey junior smiled flirtatiously at Barrett.

Barrett looked around; there were many of her plain-clothed colleagues in the bar. Freemond was with Deano across the bar. Barrett gave a little wave, Freemond ignored her, and Deano blew a kiss to annoy him. Lacey noted this, "You two not talking still?"

Barrett recalled her earlier phone call with Lacey junior. "We kept out of each other's way today. I caught up with Ged and went through the evidence."

"Tell me why you've fallen out."

Lisa giggled, "We've not fallen out, but Ray can play the father figure too much sometimes. We'll be ok by the morning." Barrett couldn't help blowing a kiss at Ray again when she caught his eye. Ray turned his back, ignoring her completely.

"So, do you think he'll turn up?" Barrett asked.

"Carnello? Of course. His ego wouldn't be able to stop him. Hence all you guys protecting Dad and me."

"You get personal protection," Barrett batted her eyelashes.

Suddenly, all the bar's murmuring stopped as the door opened and in walked Carnello. Followed by a gang of men, the big one being Tyson Frith. Murphy was the only person to move and approached Carnello. "Mr Carnello. This booth here is for your men, drinks on the house. Your guests are at the other booth."

"I'll sit with the boss!" Although Tyson was speaking low, his voice still appeared to boom out in the now silent bar.

"Thank you, Tyson, but please stay with the men. I'm only a short distance away." Carnello instructed.

Murphy looked up at Tyson, "I'll put the music on then."

Murphy did as he said, and the bar livened up again. Carnello shook Captain Ward and Dave Lacey's hands as he joined them. "Whiskey, I believe?" Lacey senior said as Carnello made himself comfortable. Pointing out a small bottle on the table Lacey senior invited Carnello to open it. Checking out the label, he turned the top, breaking the seal, and poured himself a glass.

"Black Label, you've gone up in the world, Lacey."

"Probably not as much as you, but I do ok. Legitimately of course!"

Carnello chuckled, "And I thought this was to be a friendly meeting."

Lacey smiled falsely, "Now, what gave you that stupid idea?"

"You think you're big enough to take me on after all these years? Of course, I wasn't the one to run-scared to LA." It was Carnello's turn to taunt.

"Run? I think you'll find I was learning."

Carnello looked at Ward thoughtfully then the corner of his mouth rose in a slight sneer, "How's the arm these days?"

Ward smirked, "Itching for revenge."

Carnello laughed, "It must be so frustrating to have to stick by the rules. I've never bothered personally; the prizes aren't worth the effort."

"Is that a confession, Carnello, should I get a mic for you to talk into?" Lacey continued to taunt.

Carnello thought, "You can have microphones if you like, but me? Well, I'm but a successful businessman who gave $10 million to local New York charities last year. I have nothing to hide."

Lacey smirked, "Relying on money is not always the best thing in the long term. Things change. Hell, I'm the new mayor, and I don't need any salary supplements. With the necessary... oops, unfortunate passing of the old DA the newly appointed one fortunately happens to be a high school friend of mine."

Carnello rolled his eyes before he spoke, "Such change, but businesspeople like say...me, tend to grow relationships. Hampton, the police commissioner, enjoys golf at my club. He's a valued member. Indeed, I did a course on modern networking would you believe." Carnello laughed heartily.

Lacey laughed in return, "Yes. Hampton has been a golf fanatic for a few years. I'm sure I have the power to sack him. I thought my friend here, Captain Ward, would be a good replacement."

Ward looked a bit shocked, Carnello laughed again. "You make me laugh. How's the family? I see Master Lacey over there. Can I introduce him to my protection director, Tyson Frith?"

Lacey got the threat. "You know we've not met for many years and you don't change. A bit of a dinosaur I'd say. Things don't work like that anymore."

"Really? Then let me reflect on that as I get into my new Rolls Royce. Frankly, this seat is getting rather uncomfortable. Or is it the company?"

"Ok, to business." Lacey was straight.

"At last!" Carnello replied.

"You know we have an important visitor here this coming weekend?"

"No...really? I heard it was top secret," Carnello said mockingly.

"Yes, really. From tomorrow the city will be in lockdown, more badges on the streets than you could imagine. Being my big event, I don't want it ruined by anything or anyone!"

Carnello took another swig of his whiskey. "I'm not sure that you needed to say that. I mean other business leaders and I don't want to see the city's reputation marred on the big stage. Actually, many of my business colleagues are attending the event, was my invite lost in the post?"

Lacey guffawed, then said, "No, your invite will be of a slightly different nature. It'll arrive at some point I'm sure, and it will be for a longer event. Twenty years at least."

Ward couldn't completely stifle his snigger.

Carnello caught the snigger and looked at Ward, "How's the wife?" Ward didn't rise to the bait and took a swig of his beer to disguise his disgust.

Lacey continued, "I'm glad you got to that point, Carnello. You see tonight was also to remind you of my friendship with Captain Ward. I, of course, have picked up that there are some issues around his precinct and would dearly love to see that end."

"Of course. No one would diss the President and cause trouble...I mean, be over excited this weekend. Hell, I'm even having Stars and Stripes hung outside *all* my offices."

Ward spoke, "As agreed, but the Mayor was talking long term."

"Oh, I'm sorry, I missed that. I'll see what I can do, however, I'm not sure it's anything to do with me, *officer*." Carnello said innocently with his hand on his heart.

Lacey said, "And my friend here says that some people are showing too much interest in a couple of his officers. It would very much displeasure me if anything happened to them or their families." Lacey looked towards Barrett as he said this.

Carnello looked up, he knew who Barrett was and her sitting next to Lacey junior was noted. Carnello laughed, "I'm at a loss as to what you mean but, I will say fuck you when the time comes, *Mr* Mayor. Tyson!"

Before Lacey could respond, Tyson had covered

the short distance and was next to Carnello. Lacey could sense hands-on guns everywhere in the bar, "Mr Tyson. I think your boss would like to leave now!"

Tyson smiled as he towered over the still seated Lacey and Ward. "Yes, we're off. See you soon, *Mr Mayor.*" Carnello had clearly had enough of playing nice and led his team out.

Lacey took a deep breath, "Fuck. I really thought he was going for me then. He's a big fuck."

"Yeah he is, I tried to stand, but my belly got caught on the table," Ward replied.

Lacey looked shocked, "What the fuck? I have you here to protect me, and you're too fat to even take action! Jesus, I need a beer. Murphy! Two large ones over here, now, please!"

Lacey junior stood, "Hey, sorry, Lisa, I think I want to see how Dad is, he looks shocked."

"Only if you agree to a proper date?" Barrett smiled as she rose along with Lacey junior.

"With those legs? Anytime." Lacey laughed and gave Barrett a peck on the cheek. "Friday night... remember!"

As Lacey junior left Freemond sat next to Barrett who had sat back down. "I'm sorry for acting the dick, Lisa, but you lost it and it was out of order."

Barrett clutched Freemond's hand, "I know, Ray, I'm sorry. Townsend was a good friend and I'm not handling it well. I was to be her Maid of Honour, you know."

"Oh shit, I knew you were close but…"

"Don't be. Friends like you will get me through this and get her the justice she deserves." Barrett said as she waved to the Lacey's and Ward as they left the bar.

THE ENDORSEMENT

Chapter 12

Thursday was quiet, Barrett and Freemond didn't see the captain for most of the morning but caught him in his office around 4 pm, "So, how did it go with Carnello, Captain?" Freemond asked.

"Interesting," Ward paused. "It appears Dave Lacey wants to goad the beast. He might even be looking to go to war with Carnello."

"Wow, really?" Barrett asked.

"If not a war, he wants Carnello to show his hand somehow. Maybe pushing him into a mistake. Lacey wants him."

"Could cause blood shed throughout the city, gang members and free-folk alike." Freemond noted.

Ward thought, "Maybe. But maybe that's what's needed. We won't get Carnello in the standard ways his lawyers are too good. Now, don't take this the wrong way, but Dave may have pushed Carnello to take us on. And by us, I mean us three, so you guys need to stick together and watch your backs. I've also doubled up officers in all our cars so there's less coverage across the city, but we should be safer."

"Well, that's nice of him, and you wanted to be his daughter-in-law?" Freemond joked with Barratt, wiggling his ring finger.

Barrett laughed, "I know. Fortunately, Jeff warned me what his father can be like beforehand."

"Jeff is it? I didn't think you were moving so fast; should I get Gloria a hat?" Freemond taunted.

Before Barrett could make a smart reply Ward stepped in, "Come on, guys. The Lacey's know you can look after yourselves so we're all willing targets. If Carnello is focused on us, we have the means to be supported."

"Supported?" Barrett was quizzical.

"Dave uses a special military...well, SWAT unit, for protection, They carried out most of his infamous crime lord busts in LA as well."

Freemond thought, "Many of those end in multiple deaths. Usually the villain's deaths, so that's not so bad, I guess." Freemond finished with carefree shrug of the shoulders and a smile.

Ward smiled, "That's my understanding. Dave's on our side, but rumours are he pushes the law to the end of its limit…although being mayor he could always make the law too." Ward chuckled. "Anyway, nothing will happen today or tomorrow as the world knows the President is arriving and the city is virtually in lockdown. The feds are already here checking drains and everything."

"Oh yeah. That reminds me. You've both got tickets for the bash tomorrow night. That's real friendship. Gloria and I might get a takeaway." Freemond made a point, Barrett chuckled.

Ward also laughed but pulled a card out from his top drawer. "You better look good in a tux, Ray. You and Gloria are on mine and Martha's table."

Freemond was startled, "What? You're kidding!"

Barrett chuckled, "No, we're all on Jeff's table. The limo will pick you up around 6.30 pm."

"You knew as well? Assholes!" Freemond smirked, "Hey, Captain. Can I have time off tomorrow to rent a suit?"

Ward chuckled, "You're late most days so what's the difference."

*****

Friday daytime was quiet in incident terms.

The city was a mix of tourists trying to get a glimpse of the presidential motorcade or the President himself when he entered or exited a building. Most New Yorkers saw the shutdown and over-policing a pain so stayed at home.

Barrett looked in the mirror for the fifth time. *Black is ok; it's a longer cut so it's not too 'Saturday night tart'. Yeah, this'll do.* Hearing a car pull up outside she looked out the window, the extra-long, black, shiny Limo's back door was opening and a guy in a black suit and cap was getting out.

Barrett ran down the stairs to the limo. Climbing into the limo Freemond was first in her eyeline, "My, is that you, Ray? No, it can't be, you aren't that handsome." All in the limo chuckled. Barratt turned to the other occupants, "Good evening, Gloria, Martha, Captain." After they'd shared their greetings and fussed over Barratt's outfit the limo took off.

Barrett felt like a film star when the door was once again opened when they arrived at Food & Sauce. The Press appeared to be taking pictures of anyone in a limo. A waiter checked their invites when they entered the restaurant and showed them to their table. It seemed there was more security there than at Buckingham Palace when she'd spent time in London and saw the changing of the guards. It made a change for the metal detectors to stay silent for once. There was no reason for them to be armed with the SWAT team in attendance so none of them were packing. At their table, Jeff Lacey greeted them. Hugging Barrett first and giving her a peck on the cheek he said, "You look gorgeous. Thank you for coming." Barrett blushed, having Ward and Fremond within hearing distance, she knew they wouldn't miss the sign of affection.

Lacey senior said his speech first, formally welcoming his friend, the President, and then the meal was served. Three courses in, Gloria spoke, "My, how are rich people not all fat? I can't eat another bite."

Lacey junior chuckled, "Gloria, we don't eat like this every day. Most of us have fitness instructors as well, you don't see the effort that goes on behind the scenes. Anyway, one of my favourite exercises is dancing and I've made sure that once the President has the first dance with the First Lady he'll be dancing with all three of you." Barratt, Gloria and Martha's jaws dropped and none of them said a word.

Lacey junior was true to his word' all three women danced with the President and came back glowing. Martha, the last to dance, arrived back at the table and nearly passed out with pride. "Hubby, dear, you're toast. Barmy said he would leave the First Lady for me!" all laughed.

Gloria butted in, "Hey, he said that to me as

well. The Pres is..."

Lacey junior laughed loudly and interrupted, "Ok, ladies, before first blood is drawn, I'll let you in on a little secret. I put him up to it. That's why he let you call him Barmy." Gloria and Martha laughed aloud.

"Hey!" Barrett was indignant, "He didn't say it to me!"

Lacey junior pulled Barrett close and planted a kiss on her lips before whispering, "Not even the President is getting my girl!" Barrett went red but joined in with the laughter.

The laughter was interrupted by a man in a suit, the earplug and wires in his ear gave away his status as a Secret Service operative. "Good evening, Sir. Sorry, Miss, may I have a word, Sir?"

Lacey responded, "Sure," and walked off with the man.

Barrett watched them talk then asked the returning Lacey, "Who is that guy?"

"Captain Jones. He commands Dad's personal SWAT team. They're helping protect the President for now but will be staying in New York after tomorrow."

*****

Barrett woke with a yawn and big stretch and

switched on the telly to catch the morning news. She was very happy it was a Saturday morning, and she didn't have to go into work. It was around 2 am when she'd got home. Lacey had to stay at the restaurant, so what could have been the perfect end to a perfect evening didn't entirely go to plan. Barrett called Freemond's cell, "What a great night. How's Gloria?"

"Morning, Lisa. She's thrilled. She's spent all morning trying to send the photos of us with the President to everyone we know using that What's It app."

Barrett giggled, "WhatsApp, you mean. Could Toni help her?"

Freemond laughed, "Yeah, she did in the end. I'm not going to hear the end of this. You and Lacey junior looked comfortable last night?"

Barrett blushed in the privacy of her own home. "Yeah, we were. He seems like a decent guy. What do you think of him?"

"I agree. Lacey junior seems like a decent sort. Lacey senior scares me a bit, but junior, although, he was a bit of a ladies man when he was first in his father's shadow seems to be growing up finally."

Barrett smiled, "Oh, I've just seen on the TV that the President has left, the traffic will be easier now. I'm going to visit Steph at the nursing home later if you fancy joining me."

Freemond briefly thought of Steph Mercer, John Mercers mom. "No, thanks. Gloria and I saw Steph the other week. No change, she still thinks John, even Tanya, are still alive. Poor woman. I have to get to the clothes hire shop, have you seen the prices of those suits if you don't return them in time!"

Barrett laughed, "You don't want to be paying for them, but you did look good, Ray."

Freemond laughed, "I'll pop over to Darius's father's shop later and see if he's heard anything. Tomorrow, Toni's Scott is back, he's been away for two weeks, so we've planned a family dinner. You're welcome to join us?"

"Ray. You're always on duty. Thanks for the invite but a certain Lacey gentleman has mentioned a walk along the coast for Sunday."

Freemond chuckled, "It's good to hear you so happy. Have fun and I'll see you at work on Monday, partner."

A KILLING SPREE

Chapter 13

Denice Damond got out of the car, it was her third trick of the evening even though it was only 7 pm. She took out a roll-up and decided to have a break in the alley just below the corner she worked. Walking some ten metres into the dimly lit alleyway she took a drag, closing her eyes to enjoy the moment. As she opened her eyes, her heart missed a beat in terror. She was staring at the barrel of a gun. She could see a hooded figure behind the barrel but no details. The gunman remained silent when handing Damond an envelope. Taking five steps back with the gun still raised the gunman turned and walked off.

Damond gathered herself and opened the envelope. Her eyes filled with glee, inside were dollar notes, and lots of them. She didn't bother counting them before removing the piece of notepaper from inside. Walking closer to the one light on the corner Damond read the note...

*****

The squad car pulled up outside the rundown house and Officers Kate Houlihan and Mason Janson exited the vehicle. Houlihan drew out her torch and Janson drew his nightstick.

"Robbery here? Never." Houlihan said disbelievingly as she approached the house.

"Be careful, Houls, I don't like this!" Janson shouted to his partner, placing his other hand on his still holstered gun.

Houlihan banged on the door with her torch. "NYPD, open up!"

The door opened and a woman appeared in front of Houlihan. "You called the police, a break-in?" Houlihan asked.

The woman didn't reply, smiled, then moved aside. The first shot took out half of Houlihan's head.

"Fuck!" Janson shouted as he fired every shot the cartridge contained into the hallway while trying to approach his fallen colleague. His thoughts were on the opening in front, he didn't check behind him. The first shot took out the back of his knee causing Janson to crumple to the floor. Looking up, he saw his killer...

*****

On the other side of town, the figure watched

105

as a motorbike came round the corner towards the Old Red Hooks fish building. The rider and passenger, neither helmeted, were on their own, there were no other vehicles around. The Harley pulled up outside the building. The female passenger jumped off first; the rider killed the engine and walked to the passenger who was up against the building wall. "Here? Are you kidding me? For the money I'm paying we could get a room for the weekend!"

The woman laughed flirtatiously, "The fresh air does something for me which means I can do something special for you in return."

The rider smiled, "You'd better!" With this, he grasped the woman and started tugging at her clothing. Things were really beginning to heat up until the woman froze. Looking in her eyes, he saw her terror. Turning, he could see why, a figure was standing just behind them with a large gun pointed at his face. The figure waved the gun and he moved away from the woman. "If you want my money then take it. Please, I have hundreds here!" The man pulled out his wallet and held out his cash." The figure ignored the move and shot a single bullet into his head. The woman screamed at the guy now sprawled on the floor in a pool of his own blood.

Looking back to the figure who was now pointing the gun at her. "I did what you wanted, mister.

I got Macomb here. Please don't shoot me...your note? We have a deal...right?" The figure turned and shot at the Harley's fuel tank, the bike exploded in flames as the figure took off, throwing another envelope to the woman. Damond, the woman, picked up the envelope, took the notes from the now dead Macomb's hand, and ran off.

*****

Freemond raced his car to the scene; as it was late the traffic was manageable, so Freemond was soon studying the scene. Two of his colleagues lay in pools of blood before him. He recognised both. His melancholy thoughts were interrupted, "No, Ray, not two of my men!"

Freemond turned to see the captain at his side. Ward had tears in his eyes. "Sorry, Captain. Houlihan and Janson, both shot point-blank."

They both froze in silence at the bloody scene before them when Barrett arrived, "Hi, guys. Captain, you ok?"

Ward looked at Barrett, "No, I'm not, Lisa, but let's not get into it here. Do your stuff and get my men off this grimy sidewalk. They deserve better than this."

"Yes, Captain." Barrett took a breath then ordered her forensics team into action.

Ward moved behind a police wagon with Freemond following, "Ray, this is it. I'm going over to Carnello's myself and taking him and his hood-lums down. Rally the squad."

Freemond wanted to agree but knew this wouldn't help. "Captain, you know the guys would do it for you and our fallen colleagues but it's not the way."

Before Ward could respond, his cell rang, "What, another one, you're kidding me?" Where?"

"Ray, there's been another killing at the Old Red Hooks. Casey, you take over here; Freemond you're with me."

*****

Within minutes Freemond and Ward turned up at their second murder scene of the night. Free-mond looked at the burnt-out Harley. Officer Smith approached him. "Evening, Sarge. The fire engine was called to a fire; someone on the main road called it in. When the fire service arrived, they found the body and called us."

"Thanks, Smithy," Freemond replied as he fol-lowed the captain to the body.

"No, way! Ray!" Ward stated upon looking at the body closely.

"You know him, Captain?" Freemond asked.

"No, not him. Look at the bullet wound. That's a

head shot just like the others but this one has one hell of a bullet hole!"

Freemond looked at the body then up at the Old Red Hooks sign, he'd been here before. "No, Captain, it won't be the same. Ged's on his way...here he is, let's let him do his job, he'll find out how this went down."

*****

Some two hours later at 1 am Freemond was back at the precinct. The captain was in his office with an empty hip flask. "You ok, Captain?"

Ward looked up at his friend, "Yeah, but that was hard, Ray. You ok?"

"Yeah. I'll get us some coffee."

"Thanks."

As Freemond approached the coffee machine, he met Barrett. "Anything?"

"Maybe, we have some prints on the shells but, I need some time before I'll have any definite answers. How's the captain?"

Freemond looked towards the captain's office, "He's ok, but he feels he's let the team down. Two of his men killed in one night, it doesn't bear thinking about."

Barrett looked towards Ward's office, "And the

other scene?"

Freemond thought, "I don't know. My bet is it'll be a Desert Eagle. The size of the hole couldn't be anything else. And the Old Red Hooks building to boot."

Barrett knew its significance; Mercer's first murder was at the same place and with a Desert Eagle. "Look, Ged's on that one and he's not back yet. As soon as I know anything you will too." Barrett threw a glance at Ward's office. "I suggest you get him that coffee as his hip flask is taking a battering!" With that, Freemond got busy helping sober up Ward.

HELP FROM
A FRIEND

Chapter 14

It was 10 am and Lisa had once again found herself asleep at Mercer's desk. Freemond was sleeping at his desk opposite. "What!" he screeched as someone shook him awake.

"Look!" Deano said as he pointed towards Ward's office. Barrett had also woken and now followed the pointing finger. Frank Caine had entered Ward's office. Five minutes passed, and Ward opened his office door, calling Barrett and Freemond in. As they entered Caine greeted Freemond with a good morning, then bent as if to kiss Barratt. Barrett evaded his advances.

Ward advised, "Frank has some news for us. Go ahead, Frank."

Caine replied, "I know who did the shootings last night. Apparently, they're rogue and did it without Carnello's permission. Don't ask me how I know..."

"You know who it was?" Freemond asked.

"Yeah. Frino, Damond and some girl...Bright...Molly Bright."

"Where are they now?" Barrett asked.

Caine shrugged his shoulders, "I don't know. If I did then so would Carnello and they'd be dead."

"Why rogue, and where does Tyson fit in all this?"

Caine stopped, "Wow, now I'm outa here. I'm not taking on that psycho. By the way the other murder last night, Charlie Macomb. He worked for me...and possibly Carnello?"

"How do you know about that..." Ward stopped as he saw the dickheads approaching. He continued, "We have nothing on it at present, we'll let those that need to know when we have something."

Caine looked at the approaching dickheads, "Of course, Captain. Fill me in when you can. Goodbye."

Caine passed the dickheads on his way out without acknowledging them. "The murder last night, fill us in!" Jenks was a little too direct.

"Manners detective. Let's start with good morning, shall we?"

"Good morning, Captain." Head started again reluctantly. "The Old Red Hooks murder, what's the story?" Head asked.

Ward rose from his chair, "Two of my officers were gunned down last night, and you ask about the murder of some Carnello shit-bag!"

Head took a step back, "Sorry, sir, it's procedure. The terrible murder of Houlihan and Janson appears to be by an external source and therefore for your team. The Macomb killing is a similar MO to Mercer's, and that's our side."

"Unbelievable!" Freemond was enraged, "What d'you think? John's got out of his grave and killed again?"

"Ray, keep your cool!" Ward commanded Freemond.

"Interesting. So, we are right, it had the same MO as Mercer's." Jenks smiled.

Ward sat and regrouped his senses. "Gentleman, there are no such findings as yet. Once *my* team has some results from the scene I'll advise IA if it's required. Close the door on your way out."

Head replied, "Then maybe we can speak to the new lab-rat, Ged is it?"

Barratt jumped out of her seat and went to face-off with Head, "Go near my lab without my permission, and you may have to take a long seat on a slab!"

"Cool it!" Ward commanded again. "Do you dickheads not get the message? This is my precinct, and unless you have an investigation, you're not welcome here."

Jenks turned to leave. Head stopped at the door on his way out, "Captain. You'll hear from our superiors about your lack of assistance on these matters. I may add too, if this Macomb murder is a replica of Mercer's, then your two officers here must not be allocated the case. Would you like me to make that formal?"

"I get the message. Tell your superior to come and see me personally, oh, and maybe the commissioner. Hell, let's all have dinner, and I'll bring the mayor!"

Head's face said Ward had won this round, he was just too well connected. "Yes, of course, Captain, but understand that I'm just following procedure. By the way, we'd still like to talk to Officer Dobbs; have you forgotten to pass his safehouse details on?"

Ward thought, "Yeah...I just forget. Getting old, you know. Deano! Show these gentlemen out!"

With the dickheads gone Barrett spoke, "They'll become a nuisance, Captain and at some point they're going to pull rank, even against you."

"I know. Dave has the commissioner on a string, so it won't get far at the moment when they escalate it."

Freemond joined in, "If Dobbs doesn't turn up for his appeal next week, then, by default, they'll support the initial trial hearing of police brutality. He'll go down for years."

"I know, but the stupid butt won't contact us. He's scared, really scared. Look, get all the details and, I'm sorry, but both your Sundays have been cancelled. 2 pm back here?"

"Yes, Captain."

*****

The morning went quickly, Freemond checked the crime reports of both scenes, Barrett went through the findings with Ged. Barrett was surprised when she found Ward, Freemond, Casey and Stone in her lab at 1.45 pm.

"Sorry, Lisa, I thought we'd have the meeting here. Casey and Stone will take the Old Red Hooks murder. You and Freemond continue with our officers' murders."

"Ged, please?" Barrett ordered.

"Yes, boss. Ok, Houlihan and Janson…lots of fingerprints at the property but the main ones were on the spent bullets. Frino's and a Ben Damond's prints on some spent bullets, but the others were gloved. No CCTV or eyewitnesses." Ged paused, "The Old Red Hooks murder was performed with a Desert Eagle, and it was one shot to the head. Forensics suggests Macomb was close to a woman going by the blonde hairs on his jacket. There were also fluid stains on his trousers, so I don't think full sexual intercourse occurred, but he was definitely...happy before he died, let's say."

"So, our killer is a woman?" Casey asked.

"Maybe, but, there were three sets of footprints in the dirt. One set matched the victim, the other is a high heel, which intermingled with Macomb's. The other set I would say are from a man's size eight. These were about the same distance from the body as the shot would've been taken from."

Stone spoke, "There were also coins and a wallet full of Macomb's credit cards on the floor which suggests he paid the girl...so, a prostitute, perhaps?"

"So, our killer comes across these two doing it and decides to blow his, but not her, head off?" Ward thought aloud.

"The DNA we got from the hairs tells us they belong to Denice Damond; a known prostitute who works up near Broadway," Ged informed.

"Well, thanks for that late information. Ben Damond is her brother," Freemond informed.

"Ok. Let's pick up the Damonds, Frino and this Bright woman. If we know where they are!"

"Yes, Captain." The four Detectives filed out of the lab.

"Oh, and that bloody Zola lad, find that fuck too!" Ward shouted; and then under his breath added, "I'll find Dobbs."

*****

The day saw four police raids on the houses of the named suspects none of which were home. Freemond was at the last place, Bright's apartment, and called Ward, "Hi, Captain, nothing here. She's disappeared just like the others. And no one's talking. Is it possible they've all been set up by Carnello?"

Ward replied, "Yeah, it looks that way. Funny we found the prints of those named by Caine but not the others. I feel if we don't find these kids soon, they won't be around to tell their story."

"I agree, Captain. We're on our way..."

Ward interrupted, "No, you're not. You both go home and get some rest."

A SETUP

Chapter 15

"Hi, Jeff. Yeah, we're busy. I'm sorry about yesterday can we go another time... Great, catch you later... Yeah, a quick one at Murph's, he can throw a few burgers out." Barrett smiled as she ended the call.

"Good job yesterday, Ged." She said as she headed for the squad room stairs.

At the top of the stairs, before entering the squad room, Freemond caught Barrett by the arm, "Come on. We're going out. I have a hunch." Barrett didn't say anything and followed. Freemond continued to talk on his cell. "You're sure he'll meet us...for about fifteen minutes. Thanks, Demis, I owe you one, buddy."

Once in the car Barrett quizzed Freemond, "Where we going.? What has Demis told you?"

Freemond replied, "Enyo Hollas, the Greek-gang boss will see us at his legit Statue of Liberty tourist ferry on the Westside."

Barrett had heard of Hollas, "Wow. He and his gang have been quiet for some time. Are they still in business?"

Freemond laughed. "Come on, stupid. They all grew up and have hidden behind legit businesses for years, but they can't keep the money flowing like it always has done using purely legitimate means. Hollas is no different than Carnello, he's just better at hiding it and uses less lethal means."

Barrett and Freemond were soon on the river-bus pier. They walked to an old Greek man leaning against the river railings. "Detectives, would you like a free crossing? Our statue is gleaming today in this lovely sunshine." Hollas greeted them with a big smile and shook both their hands.

"Good afternoon, Mr Hollas. Thank you for agreeing to meet us," Freemond replied.

"Hey, if my friend's son, Demis, wants something then I'll always try to help. You're looking good, Detective Freemond, did I hear you'd had a health scare?"

Freemond smiled, "Yes, I did, but I'm ok now. I'm as strong as an ox."

Hollas pretended to tap Freemond's stomach, "And nearly as big as one, my friend." With that, Hollas laughed but also tapped his own rather large belly. "So, if this visit is not for pleasure then what can I do for you?"

"We need to find Zola and the Georgio girl, and quickly. We have reason to believe that Carnello may wish ill of them," Freemond was straight to the point.

"I see," Hallos thought, "I don't have any influence on those two since they joined the wrong business, so why should I now?"

Freemond leant against the railings, "You and Carnello are business competitors. Now we have some interest in Zola and Georgio that may... let's say, provide some business information that could cause Carnello some trouble."

After a pause Hallos replied, "Maybe, but I no longer compete with Carnello; he's too public. He no longer gives us businessmen a good name," Hollas laughed loudly.

Freemond chuckled, "These are desperate times, and our side would much prefer your... quieter approach."

"And if I knew someone who could help, how would my business benefit?"

"Maybe it's time for Carnello to go bankrupt with the state's full support!"

"Always a straight guy, Detective." Hallos

looked at Barrett, "Have you been this guy's partner since the tragic Mercer case?"

"Nearly, sir," Barrett replied.

"Sir! I like this girl, Freemond," Hallos chuckled. "You know, this oaf used to think I was a bad guy. Chased my butt all over the city when he was younger. If all cops were like Freemond here the world would be a better place. Nowadays it's not about people but targets and KPI's and bonuses. Do you get bonuses for framing people these days, Freemond?"

Freemond laughed, "No, Mr Hallos, just great joy!"

Hallos joined in with the laughter. "Look I don't like to be seen to helping you guys it can be bad for business, but maybe there is a joint interest here. I'll message you if I hear anything."

"Thank you, Mr Hallos," Freemond said as he shook his hand and left.

*****

Ten minutes later Freemond pulled the car up outside a mobile coffee van. Handing Barratt a full-fat latte he made himself comfortable. "Why are we starting to do deals with these people?" Barratt asked.

"We're at a stage where we have to take each

day as it comes. Unfortunately, these people, who should all be locked up, play a part. We want our colleagues' killers and whoever is behind it all, therefore, we have to deal with them to get there."

"I agree with that, but if we catch Frino or Zola, or any of that lot really, one of them will talk."

"Really?" Freemond looked at Barratt. "All those people are more scared of Carnello and his gang than anything that justice can do to them."

"Carnello will kill them!"

"...and their families," Freemond said rather sombrely.

"Have you spoken to Casey or Stone?"

"Earlier, but they have nothing as yet."

"Could it be Mercer, or a copycat?" Barrett shrugged as she said this.

"I wish it were John, but hey, we saw him buried. A copycat? The problem is the accuracy of detail suggests it'd more likely be one of us."

Barrett sat up, "You think so?"

Freemond looked around, even though they were alone in the car. "The guys reckon it's Dobbs. He was quite involved in John's case, and he knows he'll be locked up for the Dez case."

"Wow!" Barrett cried. "I wouldn't have thought

of that."

"Well, who knows. What's worse is we think the captain's covering for him."

"So, what do we do?"

"Nothing. Let him blow all their fucking brains out." With that, Freemond laughed loudly and drove off.

*****

Tyson took the call, even though it was late, "Ok, I get it. What's Hollas got to do with this?" The caller replied but Tyson interrupted, "Come on, he was one of his, and we don't want a fight with Hallos. Set Zola up, an internal issue at the precinct would be better than a killing." After listening for a while Tyson replied again, "Ok, just timing. Zola knows where to run we just need to get some cops there. What time?"

"We'll give the snitch details about Hallos pushing his whereabouts tonight at 1 am. You'll be called to set the trap. If the trap doesn't work, kill everyone you have to we don't need Zola getting caught." The caller ended the call.

*****

"Ray, it's nearly 1 am, please!" Barrett shouted down her mobile.

"I've a lead on Zola. I know where he is. We have

a squad on their way. Get there in ten minutes, or you'll miss it. I've texted the address already." Freemond sounded revved up. Barrett jumped out of bed, dressed as quickly as she could and was on the way in minutes.

*****

Zola's burner phone beeped. "Fuck! Run, the cops are coming." With that, he and four others took off from the apartment in different directions. Zola had been told his safe route and took the first two blocks before heading towards the third. As he turned the corner he saw a police car that had just stopped some youths. Zola's movement caught Officer Smith's eye and he took chase, forgetting his partner, Officer Detrice, who was with the other youths.

Zola turned into an alley, he knew this led to his new safe house and Smith was not far behind. As Zola passed a bin he caught sight of a man hiding behind it. The man called him over. "Waste the pig!" The man said as he passed Zola a gun as Zola joined him by the bin. Zola took the weapon and looked up.

Officer Smith was nearly on him. Smith, seeing that he'd hid behind a bin, gun drawn, called, "Police, come out now or I'll shoot!"

Zola froze. The man to his right winked at him while holding out another gun, aimed at Zola.

Zola knew he only had one chance. He stood, with the gun he had raised and aimed at the cop. Officer Smith had no option. Three bullets hit Zola who fell instantly to the floor.

"Smithy, what the..." Officer Detrice had caught up with Smith. Both heard a shriek and within, what appeared to be seconds, the street started to fill with people. Smith saw a woman now leaning over the body of Zola. The woman screamed, "You've killed him. He was unarmed!"

"What?" Smith cried, "No!"

Officer Detrice grabbed the screaming woman and handcuffed her. "Everyone get back, now!" Detrice called as her eyes looked for a weapon. "Was there anyone else here?" Detrice called to her partner.

"No, I don't think so. There must be a gun. I saw a gun!" Smith was by his partner's side. Within seconds police cars were everywhere. Hearing the commotion over the radio, Barrett and Freemond knew the address they'd been headed too had been rumbled and responded to the call as well and arrived along with the other officers.

Barrett approached Smith first, "Are you ok?"

"Yes!" Smith responded shakily, then almost begged, "He had a gun, please, find the gun!"

Freemond helped Detrice pull the crying

woman from the floor. Detrice did a quick body search. "No weapon!"

Barrett noted more officers had joined them. They were holding back the crowd which was now on both sides of the alley. "Close this off, guys, it's a crime scene. Ray, please."

Freemond walked up to Smith and said, "I'm sorry, buddy, but I need your weapon, and you need to come with me."

*****

"Yes, sir, I know...thank you!" Ward slammed the phone down.

Barrett and Freemond entered his office, "Good morn...I mean, afternoon, Captain. Are you ok?"

Ward looked at the clock. It had just gone noon. "Ok! That was the commissioner, and the DA before that, and numerous press assholes before that!"

Barratt handed Ward the coffee she'd brought, "Sorry, you two worked most of last night again. What can you tell me?"

Barratt started, "No gun, Captain."

Ward froze, "No...no...Officer Smith is as straight as straight can be. I mean he's by the book! There must have been a gun. Did the woman take it or maybe toss it to someone."

Barrett advised, "It's possible, Captain but Smith and Detrice were on them fairly quickly and didn't recall seeing anything thrown. The alley's initial search shows nothing; although, the bin next to where Zola fell had a door next to it. It was locked when we were there, however, we entered the premises about half an hour afterwards and the bar owner had been cleaning the service room that the door leads to, at 2 am, which might mean something."

"Wainburg's, right?"

"Yes Captain. A very seedy joint that was open at the time, but it was cleaner in that area than all the rest."

Freemond had been listening, "So someone could have taken the gun and jumped into Wainburg's, it was a setup, Captain, must've been. They knew where Zola would run to, and the traffic offence which Smith and Detrice caught and followed before stopping the kids was just in front of the alley."

"Sounds plausible but the press are saying no gun. Smithy is in bits downstairs and the dickheads already want to charge him." Ward dropped his head, "Ok, you need to push Wainburg, and whoever the youths were in the car our guys stopped, they'll know something. I'll deal with the noise."

Ward stopped as he saw Mayor Lacey enter the office. "Hi, Dave." They all said in unison.

"Good afternoon, all. Wardy, you need some moral support at least. I'm here to help." No more needed to be said and Barrett and Freemond left the office and the station.

*****

Pulling the car up at Wainburg's, Barrett and Freemond entered the bar. "You were right, Lisa. My shoes are virtually sticking to this sodden floor. Bet the storeroom *was* cleaned last night." Approaching the bar, Freemond knew the bartender, Harry Wainburg, who was also the owner, "Good afternoon, Harry, a chat around the back, if you please?"

Wainberg didn't reply, just led the two cops to the gleaming storeroom. "So, who did you let in last night, Harry?" Freemond was not beating around the bush.

Wainberg was uneasy in his response, "No...no one. I had rats here for a while so needed to clean up...and last night was quiet, so I took the opportunity."

"At 2 am?" Barrett asked.

"Yes. I work all hours it's not a 9-5 job being a bar owner."

"So, you did the cleaning?" Freemond pushed.

"Yes, just me."

"So, if I bust your butt for hiding evidence what would that do to you and your business?" Freemond gave a mocking laugh.

"You can't do that, Detective Freemond. Cleaning is not a crime and besides the press were here most of the morning. I could claim police brutality," Wainburg was rattled.

Freemond replied cautiously "Let me advise you, then. Gangland bosses are an immediate threat. However, we are the NYPD, and we do get our man, just not always as quickly as they do. We can have the health department raid unclean bars; we can use the backing of revenue officials who can be a little overzealous in say, a run-down joint, like this."

"You threatening me, Detective?"

"Not at all. I'm educating you. I think people need to know that whatever the threat, we will win out and you should all start to look at the long term prospects of having a business in this town as well as the short term." Freemond turned on Wainburg, "You have my number. I and the NYPD are getting bored with these games, so make a change."

*****

Pulling up outside the high school just as students came out Freemond headed for two specific students. "Hey, are you Evans and Yellin?" The two students looked at Freemond, who was holding his badge up.

Yellin responded, "Yes, sir!"

Freemond smiled, "You resemble your older brother, Yellin, how is Tito?"

"He's good, Officer. Just had a kid. I'm an uncle at seventeen."

Freemond smiled, "So our guys pulled you up near Wainburg's last night. A bit late on a school night?"

"We had a free morning, so we went for a drive."

"Nice car you were driving, Evans."

"Eh...yeah."

"Just bought it that day?" Barrett asked.

"No. It's a friend's and they haven't used it for a while, so we took it out to charge the battery. It's my flatmate's...but I'm insured and everything. It's all legit."

"Yeah, we checked. So, what were you doing out that late, or more importantly, why did you stop

130

at Wainburg's?"

"We told your colleagues all this earlier. Besides we're minors so you shouldn't be talking to us without an adult or lawyer present."

"Who did you speak to earlier? We only have details of your driving offence?"

"Officer's Head and Jenks caught us as we arrived this afternoon at school." Freemond knew there was no more to be had from this.

*****

Freemond and Barrett left and headed for Demis' bar. Demis sat next to them and presented them with beers once they had taken a booth, even though it was early. "Hallos is not sure if he can help after last night. He didn't want Zola dead."

Barrett responded, "It was Hallos who got us the lead for Zola?"

"Yes, or at least he was able to get the details from his connections."

Freemond thought, "So Hallos helps us, Carnello finds out and offers us, Zola, on a plate. We have the press all over us and now Hallos is against us too?"

"Maybe not against you, but he will be weary of helping anymore."

"The Georgio girl?"

"Somehow she's been passed back to Hallos, he's good friends with her father. I'd suggest that a *'sorry we had to set up Zola but here's Georgio on a plate'* deal between Hallos and Carnello might be in order."

Barrett took a swig of her beer, "That's quick, Demis."

"Yeah. Carnello is big, but he wants you guys, not the other gangs, so keeping them happy is important to him."

"Hallos won't give us Georgio?"

"Sorry Ray, he'll assume you can't protect her so won't go for it. She'll probably be back in Greece by tomorrow."

Once they returned to the car Barrett spoke, "So the dickheads got to the kids first?"

"Yeah," Freemond replied. "Probably to make sure the correct story's on record.

"It all seems a bit fast, a bit messy."

"Yeah. It's not normally Carnello's style, he thinks things through in depth usually, but this time he seems to have taken steps without filling in all the gaps. Wainberg and the kids in the car will talk once we pull them in formally."

Barratt smiled, "And Dobbs and his killing?"

"Strange, it seems to have taken a back seat. Macomb is a gang member but not respected or high up, so I'm not sure where this fits into things." Freemond replied.

"You know Ged was asked to pull John's gun from storage and check it was still there. And check if it'd been used. Which it hadn't, obviously."

"Maybe it's not Dobbs. Maybe it's Carnello faking a copycat to fuel the press?" Freemond said without conviction.

"Maybe, but it's not taken off this time, it's lost in all these other dealings."

Freemond thought, "Look, you're out with young Lacey tonight. Have a good time, and let's hope these canaries sing under real interrogation tomorrow."

Barrett smiled and thought of her quick burger date with the handsome, young Lacey, later.

*****

Freemond came out of the interview room and banged his fists on his desk as he sat down. Barrett had been waiting in Mercer's chair for some time, "So, how are the interrogations going?"

Freemond grimaced, "The two kids are polished, it was all a coincidence and Wainberg is not moving. He's asked about police protection, though."

"Is that why the dickheads are with him now?"

Freemond looked towards where Barrett was pointing. He immediately stood back up and headed for the interview room but was stopped by Captain Margent as he went to enter. "Sergeant Freemond. My men are doing their jobs, leave them alone with the suspect."

As Margent spoke, Ward came out of his office, "What's going on?"

Margent replied, "Ah, Captain Ward. I've been looking forward to seeing you. My men are talking to the gentleman about police protection. I, of course, wish to see you about your men." Margent looked at Freemond.

"Ray, leave them alone. Captain Margent, come into my office." Ward directed.

Freemond rolled his eyes, turned and went to the coffee machine. Returning to his desk with a coffee, he sat down with a growl. Barrett asked, "Is Margent on the take?"

"Yes. Well, he was when he was less senior, but now he allows his men to get away with things instead."

Barrett grimaced, "Is IA the most corrupt squad in the NYPD?"

Freemond chuckled, "Sometimes it seems so, but isn't your boyfriend and soon to be father-in-law doing anything about this?"

Barrett ignored the jibe about the mayor. "He's not my boyfriend...yet! He may have mentioned changes in IA, even regarding the commissioner."

"Time. It all takes time, and yet the criminals don't seem to worry."

An hour later with the dickheads gone and all the interviewees sent home, Ward pulled Barrett and Freemond into his office. "We've learnt nothing from the interviews with either witness. Neither want to take the State's evidence route with police protection, even if they knew anything."

"And you're not surprised?" Barrett asked.

Ward looked around as if to check no one else was listening, "I know Wainburg, he was a good man but couldn't make a decent living. Buying that shit joint was never his intention, but a man and his family have to live." Ward paused, "I caught him on his way back from the john and...well... suggested he needed to start playing ball for the good of the community. All he said was the new typhoon was not being messed with."

"Tyson Frith?" Freemond checked.

"That's the one. It seems this Frith has a bigger reputation than the last. No one will talk. Fancy a quick one at Murphy's to end this awful week?"

ANOTHER ASSASSINATION

Chapter 16

It was a rainy Saturday morning and Tyson Frith got out of the car outside the cemetery; leaving his lieutenants at the gate, Tyson walked through 100m of headstones. Soon he was looking down at his brother's grave. Standing still with his head bowed he prayed for his lost younger brother. He didn't notice the figure come from behind, but he did hear the click of a gun. As he turned, a Desert Eagle stared him in the face. Tyson couldn't make out the figure, who was hooded, wearing dark clothing, dark mask and gloves. He considered pulling his weapon, but he knew it was too soon. If he did it now the figure would shoot before it had even left the holster. *Stall for time,* he thought. "Who are you? You're not the one that put my brother here?" The figure didn't respond, Tyson saw the gun lower a little. "If you were going to kill me, you'd have done so already. What do you want?"

The figure didn't move but spoke with a gravelly voice, "Who's your boss?"

Tyson couldn't make out who the voice could possibly belong to it was so distorted. "I'm my own boss!" He replied.

The figure lowered the gun a bit more; Tyson felt a little easier but had erred on the side of caution and moved his hand towards his weapon. "It's not Carnello who brought you here, was it?" The figure asked.

"Fuck you!" Tyson suddenly went for his gun, dragging it out of the holster he managed to get his finger on the trigger before the figure's gun rose and hit him with two shots, one to the chest and one to the head. He crumpled at the feet of the figure.

*****

"Holy fuck!" Freemond stared wide-eyed next to Barrett and Ward looking down at Tyson Frith's body which had landed virtually straight on top of his brother's grave.

"What do you think?" Ward asked.

Barrett replied, "With this rain and mud it's unlikely we'll get any evidence. My initial feeling is his goons caused much of this mess as they tried to save him before calling us." Barrett took a step closer and knelt next to the body.

Ward spoke, "Look, this is Ged's case. If it could be our Desert Eagle guy you need to leave him to it, Lisa."

Before Barrett stood she read the words on the gravestone. Once standing she spoke aloud, "I can guess why he was here; it's not the anniversary of his brother's death...it's his brother's birthday."

Freemond scanned the headstone, "That's a good call, Lisa."

"Hi, Ged, all yours!" Ward and the others moved out of the way towards the gate. "The press!" Ward added, looking toward the mass of bodies already at the gate.

"It's awful, Captain, but we can't stop them." Barrett said in reassurance.

"Look, you two enjoy what's left of your weekend. Casey and Stone are on this one. I'll...ride the trouble again." With that Ward left to talk to the press.

"I feel so sad for him. No matter how much he's paid, I wouldn't want his job." Barrett shook her head as she watched him walk away.

Ray looked towards his captain, and replied, "Me neither. The last few weeks have been harsh on him. At least with this motherfucker out of the way we may get some answers. Look, I'm shopping this afternoon with Toni, fancy joining us?"

"No, thanks, Ray. I'm going to crash on the sofa today and save up my energies for my day with Jeff tomorrow."

*****

Sunday morning came; Jeff Lacey took Barrett out in a hired convertible.

Freemond was taking in a game with his son-in-law. "Great goal, that!" Scott shouted, "I need a drink."

"I'll get them lets sneak out now before the break, the bar will be quieter," Freemond replied.

Walking towards the quiet bar, Scott looked at Freemond. "You look tired, Dad." Scott called his father in law Dad, as a fond gesture.

Freemond smiled, "It's been a long few weeks."

"Are you ill again?" Scott was concerned.

"No. Physically, I feel ok but I'm mentally exhausted. Look, I know you were sacked, but you never gave me the real details. Didn't you appeal to Frank Caine directly?"

Scott looked uneasy, "Look, Dad, that's history. I'm working again so it's all good. Yes, being away from Toni and Charlotte hurts but we'll get by for now."

"You know there are people, me included, who think Caine called you off for a specific reason. Tell me what happened."

"I'm sorry, Dad. I never wanted to tell you because I knew it'd hurt you. Caine basically said that you and the force messed up his sister's case, and me being related to you meant it was partly my fault too so he wouldn't help me."

"Why didn't you tell me then?"

"Because you were ill, and besides, it's hurt you, like I thought it would, I can see it in your eyes."

"It hurts me a lot to think that something I've done has hurt you, my family, but that isn't a good enough reason to suffer it by yourself."

"Look, Dad, me and Toni are strong. We are and we will get through this. There's a world outside of New York. Maybe we could all move somewhere else, together?"

"Yes, maybe. I need the john," Freemond turned hearing a loud cheer, "sounds like someone's scored."

*****

"You're quiet, Ray, busy weekend?" Deano asked.

"Sorry, Deano. I've been listening to the news and all the madness around Frith and the others' deaths has got me all melancholy."

Deano sat at Mercer's desk, "It's a crazy world, and it's all looking like we're behind it."

Freemond smiled at his friend, "It seems that way. What have Casey and Stone said about the murder?"

Deano gave a wink, "You know I can't tell you… but…they have nothing of significance; same big gun both times, no CCTV evidence or any other clues found. It's Mercer all over again."

"Don't be silly, Deano. Next, we'll be checking his grave."

"Afternoon boys, who's grave?" Barrett smiled as she approached.

Deano smiled back and got up to let Barrett take his place, then he walked to his desk.. "How was your day with Lacey junior?" Freemond asked.

"Good. He's a nice guy."

"Deano says we have no more on the Desert Eagle killer, or on our cases."

Barrett thought before answering, "He's right. However, no one seems to want to find Dobbs so maybe they're stalling."

"Is there any evidence it's Dobbs?"

"No. But he's still missing as is his family which makes him look guilty."

"Maybe."

Barrett quizzed, "Is Frith been taken out going to help us?"

Freemond thought, "Carnello's obviously a threat but without Frith people may be more easily persuaded to offer up information. The bad guys will now think we have teeth again."

Barrett giggled, "As if the NYPD never had teeth."

Freemond laughed, "Look, I'm going to wind Wainburg up again, do you want to join me?"

*****

"Well, that was useless. No change there." Barrett announced in defeat as they got into the car outside of Wainburgs.

"I'm not sure, he was less tight-lipped, and his face when I said Tyson couldn't hurt him anymore gave something away. I think Tyson was behind the bin on the night of Zola's death," Freemond supposed.

"Wow, you do pick things up. But even if he told us, Tyson's dead, where would that leave us?"

The radio crackled, Barratt picked it up. "Thanks, Deano." We have a sighting of Denice Damond, she's heading for Broadway."

Within minutes the car pulled up at the Broadway and Times Square junction. Barrett and Freemond jumped out. "There, Ray! The red hat!" Both detectives moved towards the woman in the hat. It was Denice Damond.

Freemond didn't need to flash his badge, Damond knew him, and pleaded, "Come on guys, it's the start of the week and I need some money!"

"You've been away, Denice?" Freemond quizzed.

"Yeah. Relatives in Boston. Got back last night."

"Spending money?" Barrett quizzed.

"Hey, good looking, you could change jobs!" Damond teased, eyeing up Barratt.

Barrett laughed, "No. I prefer my type of handcuffs, thanks," as she held her handcuffs out to Damond.

"Ah fuck, you're arresting me?"

"You know the drill, let's go!" Barrett cuffed Damond and led her to the car.

*****

Barratt and Freemond entered Ward's office mid conversation between Ward and Stone.

"What's she said?" Ward continued without pausing.

"She admits she was at the murder scene doing a trick and took the cash from Macomb's wallet before fleeing, she was scared," Stone advised.

"And our killer, did she see him?"

"Yeah. Same MO as Mercer. Hooded, built, dark mask covering his face, so she was unsure of anything else. Said he didn't talk, just shot Macomb and let her go."

"Nothing else?" Barrett asked.

"She said he wasn't that tall. John was, so it's not him, obviously."

Ward grimaced, "I'm not sure of that. The dickheads are looking to exhume his grave." Barrett and Freemond grimaced. "Stone, hold her tonight, and see if we can find her brother. You two go home." Ward shooed Barratt and Freemond out of his office.

INTERESTING DEVELOPMENTS

Chapter 17

The next day was just as quiet, Barrett and Freemond had been looking for the missing Frino and Bright, and even without Frith in the background, people didn't talk. Around 3 pm they got an unexpected call to meet Carnello at his office. Upon approaching the office, they bumped into Caine on his way out.

"Good afternoon, detectives. Lisa." Caine welcomed them.

"Is it?" Freemond said as he barged past Caine.

"What was that about?" Caine said as he looked after Freemond.

"Maybe he can see the shit you really are, like I have." Barrett was taking no prisoners and walked by Caine without another word.

Within a few minutes, they were in Carnello's

opulent office on Madison Avenue. Both cops rejected the drinks offered by Carnello. "Look, Detectives, all this unfortunate business and your bosses not talking to me either, sending their minions to do their duties instead?"

"Thanks for the compliment, Mr Carnello, but you called us?"

Carnello sat and looked at Barrett. "So, you're Lacey junior's new girl then?"

Barrett smirked, "My relationship, if there is one, has nothing to do with you, Mr Carnello."

Carnello smirked, "If your guy's father won't speak to me, then maybe you will. I have a message for him."

"And that message is what?"

"Well, with all the recent developments which have been of interest, I'm not sure it's good publicity for certain firms. So, if, and that's a big if, I did my bit to cool things, then maybe daddy Lacey would calm down his side?"

Freemond chuckled, "Getting cold feet, Mr Carnello?"

Carnello laughed and took a drag on his cigar. "You get me wrong. I have no idea about the present commotion. Although, seeing the police in such a media mess does entertain me, it has gone on too long though."

Freemond thought, "If that's the case, then maybe we could find Frino or Bright?"

Carnello paused, "I don't know what you mean; however, if there were an agreement to be had then maybe."

Barrett spoke, "So you'd be willing to talk to Lacey and help us resolve the murder of our colleagues?"

Carnello shook, "Oh, so direct! Freemond, educate your partner. Good afternoon to you both."

*****

Barrett and Freemond went to Demis' to discuss these events. Barrett looked up from her drink, "Maybe Carnello isn't behind it all?"

Freemond waited for people to move away from their booth before continuing, "It's possible, however, with Frith gone maybe he's just pulling back. Although, I think Lacey has stirred him up. Maybe Carnello's finally scared, maybe he's met his match?"

"Ok, if so, who could it be?"

Demis sat down with two whiskey shots before Barratt finished, "You'll need these, I have some news. I had a call from the man himself. He's spooked."

"And?" Barrett asked.

Demis "He says, if he hands in the main guy responsible for all this, you need to give him a deal!"

"Why didn't he tell us half an hour ago when we were with him?"

Demis laughed as he looked at Freemond, "He's unsure of you, Ray, and called me to make sure you both got the message. Especially you, Lisa, for Lacey."

"I got the message. Who is it?"

"Frank Caine. He's behind it all. He wants to get back at the NYPD and specifically the captain and you two for the death of his sister."

"I knew it," Barrett stated. "The fuck's been pretending to help us all along without actually doing anything just to gain our trust."

"It all makes sense," Freemond added. "Are you sure? Does he have that power?"

"It appears his initial plans, the media crap and ruining the reputation of the precinct, were of interest to Carnello. He actually saw it as fun. However, the introduction of Tyson Frith by Caine changed the dynamics and that's when the murders started... I'm not sure Carnello approved them. Now it's out of hand and it appears Caine is trying to take over Carnello's mob. Macomb was a lot more respected within the gang than you guys knew. With Macomb and Frith's men on his side who knows he might have enough power to overthrow Carnello?"

"So, we're to do Carnello's dirty work for him?" Barratt rolled her eyes.

Demis put a finger to his lips, "Look, Carnello knows you'll listen to me. Give him a day or two to provide the evidence, but he needs Lacey to agree to a deal. That's where you come in, Barrett."

"Ok. You know Lacey senior has no time for Carnello, so I'm not sure it'll work."

"That's what's spooking Carnello. He's scared of Lacey. Boy, when the biggest gangster gets a badge it isn't good for us honest crim...I mean, ex-criminals." Demis ended this with a big laugh. Barrett and Freemond joined in with the laughter.

*****

The next morning came and went by the time Barrett and Freemond were able to advise Ward and Lacey of their conversations with Carnello and Demis. Both were happy with the news but were tied up in meetings and press conferences so couldn't take the next step. The game would continue for now. Barrett understood this and stood with Freemond watching one of the news feeds. "The captain can hold his own on TV, don't you think, Ray?"

"Yeah. Not as well as Lacey, obviously." Freemond responded.

Barrett noticed her partner was looking a little distracted, "This is good news, right? We'll get Caine now, surely?"

"Yeah. But what will he get? A lifetime in jail or even less, or even nothing at...what...the...fuck?" Freemond froze as he looked at the screen.

Barrett looked up to see Dobbs walking up to the camera while Captain Ward was talking live on air. The microphones caught Dobbs saying, "Captain, this is all a setup. I'm happy justice will prevail, please take me in."

Ward called two uniforms over, they took Dobbs away in handcuffs, live on TV. The Press went mad, *"Is this the police vigilante that everyone was looking for..."*

"Ray. Did Dobbs call you?" Barrett asked.

"No. I had no idea. Wow, he's got some balls." For the next hour or so Barrett and Freemond tried to find out what was going on. All the captain would say was that all was in hand and he'd see them the following day.

"It's been an interesting day, Ray. I wonder why the captain is being so secretive. Let's hope tomorrow will bring Caine in, at least."

Freemond looked at Barrett, "Yeah, interesting indeed. See you tomorrow."

*****

Freemond did not take his usual route home. His head was saying *No!* But his heart was saying, *Yes!* And he sat outside Caine's office block on Park. Freemond knew that if Carnello supplied the evidence Caine would be lost in lawyers or would run. Freemond wanted to say his bit at least. After ten minutes sat in the car weighing up whether he should say his piece or not, he decided and went to get out when he saw Caine exit the building and get into his limo. Freemond followed the limo as it left the city centre and went out of town. The limo drove a few miles then stopped outside a motel. Freemond thought this was odd, and pulled into the car park too, not noticing the car behind that had also been following them.

Caine got out of the car, said something to his chauffeur, and the limo pulled off. Caine looked up at the motel and took the short flight of stairs to the first floor. Some six doors along, he knocked and entered. Freemond couldn't tell who had opened the door, so he sat and waited.

*****

"Your call was a surprise." Caine said to the woman in front of him.

Barrett smiled, "Why?" As I said on the phone. Lacey is as big a criminal as...Carnello."

Caine smiled, "So you've seen through him already?" as he loosened his tie.

"Look. Maybe we got off on the wrong foot." Barrett flashed a lot of cleavage as she walked towards the room bar. Pulling out a bottle and a pair of glasses, she turned, "Drink?"

"Why not. You look good in a skirt. You should wear them more often." Caine flirted.

Barrett smiled, "I've done some soul searching and...well...how you've acted is understandable following what Mercer did to your sister. And...well...with a copycat around I was hoping that I could persuade you to work with us properly."

Caine laughed, "Properly?"

Barrett chuckled, "Look, although your assistance is helpful it's taking time. We want whoever's behind all this now. The force is breaking up; it's going to cause my captain, my friend, to have a heart attack!"

Caine couldn't hide his pleasure, "Wow. I mean...look, how about we talk about it later, and you show me how thankful you could be if I did help more?" Barrett walked up to Caine and put her hands over his groin, squeezing his genitals.

Caine looked up, "Oh boy, you really want it this time... Wait!" He grabbed Bennett's hand and removed it, "Is this a trap?"

"No, this is the place you suggested. I've only been here for about ten minutes. You can check with the motel guy. I'm sure he saw me pull up." Releasing her hand Barrett put her hand back on Caine's groin and massaged its length. Caine groaned but put his arms around her and searched for a tap through her clothes. Interesting he thought, *if it's there it must be tiny, this outfit isn't exactly going to cover a heck of a lot.* "Look, why don't you check the bed or anywhere else for that matter. I'm going to go freshen up." Barrett whispered in Caine's ear.

Caine smiled, "Let me go first!" He said as he went to the bathroom. Barrett rifled through her bag while she waited. Caine came out of the bathroom, which he'd thoroughly checked for hidden devices. "I'm fresh, now, let me have that drink, I'm parched."

Barrett smiled as she held out her arm, draped in a lacy item of lingerie, "I'll slip into this while I'm in there!" Caine's paranoia was completely forgotten as he watched Barratt's bottom disappear behind the bathroom door.

Inside the bathroom, Barratt opened the blind, lifted the sash window and leant out. Grabbing onto a rope she pulled a rucksack into the room.

The top bodysuit inside fitted over the skimpy top she was wearing; the big trousers hid the short skirt and the four pairs of socks inside the size eight boots made them fit well enough. Last came a mask, gloves, and a hooded top.

Caine was stood at the table choosing a beer. On the table was the whiskey Barratt had gotten out for them both. *Whiskey, Black Label, I didn't realise Barratt drank whiskey, interesting.* He heard the bathroom door open and turned in readiness for an exciting night...but froze in horror instead. A figure was standing in front of the bathroom door, a Desert Eagle in hand, aimed straight at him. "What? I mean, what the fuck's going on? Who the fuck are you?" Caine backed into the table, sweat beading on his forehead. The figure pulled up the mask. "Barratt? What's going on?" Caine exclaimed in disbelief.

"You son of a bitch. You raped me!"

Caine recalled, "No, I didn't! You wanted it as much as I did."

"Is that why you had to drug me?"

"No. It was a fun drug, it made it more fun. You had fun...right? Come on, Lisa, stop pretending. You're no Mercer!" Caine was moving towards the door as he spoke.

"Stay still. Don't bet on it, Caine. You've been behind the mess with the force all along. My

155

friends, my colleagues' careers, the troubles, the murders for fuck sake. You got Freemond's son-in-law sacked. Have you got any idea how much stress that puts on a young family?"

Caine was looking less shocked and more annoyed now, "Come on, Lisa, that's silly, you have no proof!"

"Really? Then why does your boss want to hang you so much? Carnello is telling on you!"

"What? No, you're bluffing. Put the gun down and we can talk. Hell, I'll hand Carnello over now if you want!"

Barrett took a step forward and smiled, "Help us like you have for the last couple of years? No, thanks!"

"Come on, Lisa. I have real dirt on Carnello. He'll get the chair!"

"Macomb was to be your best-man; I recall you telling me that if you ever married he'd be your first choice." With a strong note of venom in her voice Barratt took a step forward. "I was to be Townsend's maid of honour."

Finally, the penny dropped, "Fuck you, bitch. Townsend wasn't killed for that she was just..."

Barrett interrupted, "A what? A cop doing her job so rich fucks like you can play with her life?

Calling in killers like Tyson to help?"

"'Ok. Ok. Pulling in Tyson was a mistake; things got out of hand; I should have known." Caine stopped having realised what he had just said. "I mean. Fuck, Lisa, we can sort this out." Caine begged, seeing Barratt's finger move onto the trigger and the barrel of the gun take aim. "Mercer murdered my sister, what would you have done?" Barrett smiled, the first shot hit Caine in the groin, and he crumpled to his knees, the second shot exploded his head all over the wall behind. Barrett pulled down her mask, grabbed the rucksack and headed for the door; the shots would have been heard.

Freemond, hearing the shots ring through the complex, jumped from his car along with Stone and Casey who were jumping out of theirs. All three officers made towards the motel until Stone shouted, "Ray! Stay there! This is our case!" Stone and Casey ran full speed up the motel stairs. Freemond stood still and watched as a door swung open along the first-floor walkway and a hooded figure all in black came out. Stone also saw the figure as he reached the top of the stairs and quickly took cover as two bullets came his way but thankfully flew above his head. By the time he looked up the figure had jumped from the first-floor walkway onto a car roof, then onto the carpark before taking off in the direction of the other side of the building.

Freemond took off, chasing the figure to the back of the building. The figure entered a forested area with deep cover. Freemond didn't stop to think about backup and followed. The figure looked back and reached for the gun but hesitated and put it away again. The distraction caused the figure to fall. Freemond was quickly on top of the prone, face-down figure. The Desert Eagle, having fell out of the undone holster, was in view on the floor in front of them.

"Freeze you motherfucker, or I'll shoot!" Freemond commanded.

The Figure stopped moving and retrieved a hand that had reached for the gun. "Don't shoot, Ray. It's me!"

Freemond was shocked, reached down and ripped off the hood covering the figure's face, "Lisa! How?...why?...what the fuck?" Keeping his gun raised as the figure turned over and sat up. Barrett smiled at her friend. "No, Lisa. No, it can't be you!" Freemond did not know what to say.

Barrett heard voices calling for Freemond. "That's Stone and Casey. Let me go, Ray, please. I'll explain later!"

"Fuck. Get out of here and take that thing with you!" Barrett smiled as she picked up the Desert Eagle and took off.

Freemond came out of the bushes out of breath; Casey was the first to his side. "Ray, are you ok, did you get the guy?"

"I'm fine, Case, I'm fine. No! He went...in that direction!" Pointing to the woods in the opposite direction to where he thought Barrett would have gone.

"Fuck. I'm not going in there. The uniforms and helicopter will be here shortly. Let's get you a drink or something. You look beat."

*****

Ten minutes later Freemond was outside the motel sat against his car's hood, a drink in hand. Ward and Ged, having just arrived, joined him. "What the fuck are you doing here?" Ward asked.

"I...I don't know, boss. What the fuck were Casey and Stone here for?"

"I thought Caine might have been told and might run so they were staking him out until we arrested him...wait, I'm asking the questions! Why are you here?"

"I was going to give him a mouthful before he got arrested, that was all," Freemond said rather feebly.

Ward looked at his detective. "No matter. Ged, come with me. Is your boss...don't bother." Ward caught sight of Barrett heading towards them. "Barrett, look after Freemond!"

Barrett hobbled as she approached Freemond. Freemond looked at his friend, then at all around the chaos of the other colleagues and witnesses outside the motel. "Not here," he said quietly to Barrett. Barrett smiled and went to the motel room, only to come back shortly after to look at a car parked in the car park.

Freemond caught Casey, "Hey, what's going on?"

Casey stopped, "You sure you're ok, buddy?"

"Yes. Just out of breath."

Casey advised, "Frank Caine's in the motel room, head blown off. Ged is picking up the evidence. It looks like there was someone else in the room as there are two glasses out. Barrett's not allowed on the case as it's too close to Mercer's MO. The owner said he saw a woman in a big coat with black hair and sunglasses get out of the car and go to the room earlier."

"Didn't she get a key?"

"No, she must have known it wasn't locked. The owner had agreed with Caine to open the room earlier and watch who went in. Obviously she was a whore, but where the killer came into this we don't know."

Casey moved off to continue his work, and Ward returned to Freemond. "So, the CCTV shows a woman but, it could've been anyone inside that room; they don't show the doors closely enough for us to work out any more details. Strangely there was a rope outside the bathroom window suggesting someone could've climbed in or out, but then where is the woman? If she went into that room at all?" Ward said aloud.

Barrett hobbled up to the two colleagues. "Are you ok, Lisa?" Ward asked, noticing the slight limp.

"I'm fine, Captain. I twisted my ankle when I got in the car in a hurry. I have some bits from the car, looks like a wig and gloves. Could a woman be our killer?"

"Not from the description Casey, Stone and our buddy here gave us. Muscled was what I heard."

"Look, you're whacked, and you're injured. Both of you get out of here, it's Casey and Stone's case now."

*****

Barrett followed Freemond who did not stop at the station but kept driving; Barrett guessed where he was going. Arriving at the cemetery, Barratt hobbled out of the car and followed behind Freemond as he walked to Mercer's grave. Without speaking he sat at the bench nearby, Barrett joined him. "I'm sorry, Ray," Barrett started.

"Lisa. I can't believe you shot three people in cold blood."

"Yes. With Dobrovskie's Desert Eagle too. It's in the trunk of my car as well as the costume."

Ray shook his head. "You killed three people. How many more if I don't stop you?"

Barrett thought, "None. I wanted Macomb and Caine. I guessed, as you probably did, he was behind everything a while ago. He was playing around with the captain, that hurts. He was taking the mickey out of us and…he raped me."

Freemond was taken aback, "What! When, I mean? Fuck!"

"A few weeks back. I can't believe I'm saying this. We dated. But I was always wary of him so we never…got together like that. And the other week he asked me out for dinner, just to talk things over he said, and he drugged me."

Anger rose in Freemond's chest, "And you didn't tell us?"

Barratt buried her face in her hands, tears muffling her voice. "Since John's been gone I've been feeling more and more like he did; how the system let him and us down again and again. When everything happened, I couldn't shake it."

Freemond looked at his crying colleague, "Macomb? Tyson Frith?"

Barrett couldn't stop crying, " I did the rape kit myself. All three had had me that night, and I had no clue and no say in the matter."

Freemond was horrified, the anger turning to tears. He put his arm around his friend's shoulders and hugged her.

THE MIGHTY FALL

Chapter 18

The next morning, seeing Barrett enter the squad room Ward called her and Freemond into his office. "Good morning, guys. How's the leg, Barrett?"

"It's ok, Captain. I've strapped it up."

Ward told them to sit. "The report states that Freemond was part of the stakeout. Casey and Stone will verify it...they think you were going to relieve them."

Freemond raised his head sharply, "Wow, Captain, that's unexpected."

Ward looked at Freemond. "Look, Ray. I'm not sure what you had to do with this, but you were obviously not the killer, and we don't need questions asked."

Freemond smiled, "And Dobbs?"

"Well, I would've sworn he was the killer but, he was under arrest when it happened. Dave Lacey is having a word with the DA to ensure his appeal will go ahead."

"And our Desert Eagle friend?" Barrett asked.

"With Caine and both Friths out the way, hopefully, he'll go away too; obviously we'll continue to investigate, but there is no...let's say...appetite to get him."

Freemond briefly looked at Barrett before saying, "I would agree with that, but will the press?"

Ward smiled, "Dave will have the commissioner changed very shortly. Dave has school friends who are now Head Hacks, so he'll control the press. And he's planning an event this evening that should help."

"Wow, what?" Barrett was intrigued.

Ward smirked, "Finally Dave has some information on Carnello. Hell, the whiskey bottle and glass at Caine's murder scene have Carnello's prints on them, no idea how but they are there, clear as day."

Freemond was shocked, "No. That can't be. It couldn't have been...ouch!" Freemond yelped as Barrett kicked his shin behind the desk. "I mean, how could it have been?"

"It's unlikely from your description of the suspect, but the evidence says he was there even if he wasn't the killer. Anyway, this and the rest of the evidence has been given to Dave and it's enough to raid Carnello's house."

"He's going to get Carnello!" Barrett exclaimed.

Ward had a big smile, "Yes! You two will buy me a drink at 8 pm tonight at Murphy's. I've booked the booth nearest the TV. Obviously, this is top secret for now!"

"Of course!" Barratt and Freemond were both grinning broadly when they left Ward's office.

*****

At 8 pm the three colleagues were sat in the reserved booth at Murphy's, drinks at the ready, live local news on. The TV showed the police raiding an expensive New York suburban residence across town, Carnello's mansion. Although the press and helicopters surrounded the grounds there was no way they could see the elite SWAT team inside.

Captain Jones led his men through the house; two guards had already been silenced with silenced gunfire; he led his team to Carnello's office. One of the team tried the door, it was open which surprised them all. Jones signalled, and after the entrance had been swept for trip wires, he and two other officers entered; the others remained at the door.

The room was empty apart from Carnello who was sitting at his desk. Carnello stood with his arms raised. He had been watching the raid on his own CCTV system. "This won't stand up in court. Tell Lacey to go fuck himself," Carnello smirked as he said this.

Jones laughed in reply, the two other officers grabbed Carnello. Carnello tried to lash out but was being held. He saw the small gun placed close to his head. Jones smirked and pulled the trigger. Carnello hit the floor. Jones placed the gun in Carnello's hand and rearranged his body as though he'd shot himself.

Mayor Lacey was outside the mansion with the press. He addressed the crowd after one of his assistants whispered in his ear. "Ladies and gentlemen of the press. My special unit was called here today to investigate various criminal activities, including the possible involvement in yesterday's horrendous killing of Frank Caine..." Lacey paused while the crowd whispered amongst themselves. "It would appear that Mr Carnello, the homeowner, has taken his own life during the raid. We can't confirm his guilt or his innocence at this time, but we will continue our investigations and update you when we can." With that, Lacey said his goodbyes and left.

*****

"What the fuck! Didn't know Carnello had it in him." Freemond exclaimed.

Ward lifted his glass, and Freemond and Barrett raised theirs. "I told you they'd get the mother-fucker. I'm sure they'll find enough evidence to ex-onerate the NYPD. Happier times are here, team!"

Barrett and Freemond both smiled, "Happier times!" They said in unison as they downed their shots.

"So, is this finally over, Captain?" Barrett asked.

"I'd say so. It won't bring back our losses but we're confident we'll find enough information in the mansion to explain many things and tie up many mysteries. And I believe Dave's team will get the whereabouts of those we're missing from any-one who is left in there." Ward chuckled.

About fifteen minutes later, Demis entered the bar and joined them in the booth. "Hey, Demis, what're you doing in Murphy's bar? Checking out the competition, feeling threatened?" Freemond baited.

Demis smiled and waved at Murph behind the bar before addressing Freemond, "Ray, healthy competition is never a bad thing, and New York is a big place. Besides the captain invited me."

Ward smiled at Demis, "You know about Carnello?"

"Yeah! Wow."

"And Hallos, you have spoken to him yet?"

Demis smiled, "Five minutes ago. He's shocked about Carnello. It seems things will definitely settle down now, especially after his meeting with the young Lacey. He thinks with his competition out of the way you'll find all those you want." Barrett and Freemond smiled.

Murph sat at the booth placing a tray of fresh drinks on the table. "Big day, big news!"

Demis downed his first shot, and said, "Yes, sure is!" Then, looking at Ward, he asked, "The figure guy, anything on him?"

Ward didn't notice the look that passed between Freemond and Barrett as he replied, "Well, it remains an open case. Let's see if anything comes out in the wash."

Demis gave a quizzed look, and said, "Maybe this cheap booze has got to me already, but..." pausing to smirk at Murph, "am I the only one to wish that Merce was not dead & sitting with us now?"

Barrett shifted in her seat uncomfortably, Ward caught the movement and asked, "Lisa?"

"Someone walked over my grave," she explained as she shook it off. Addressing Demis she added, "Sorry, but John is very much dead and sadly he's not returned from the grave." Barrett smiled sadly.

Freemond took a quick look at Barrett before speaking, "We'll uphold the law. As the captain says, we'll see what comes out in the wash. However, my guess is I'm not sure we'll hear from him again; Carnello's mob seemed to be his target for some reason."

Ward gave Freemond a quizzical look. Before he could say something Murph raised his glass, "To Mercer. He would be happy that Carnello is dead and gone. Rest in peace, friend!" They all raised their classes and loudly toasted Mercer's memory then downed shots.

Ward looked around the table, smiled and said, "Maybe I'm already drunk but it sure feels good to be here with you all, to friends and colleagues."

Demis chuckled, "Keep it low boss man, some of us have a reputation to keep. Friends is a bit much!"

As everyone laughed Ward lifted another glass and waited for his friends to raise theirs before shouting, "I love New York!"

The End

Novellas by Ken Kirkberry:

Sci-fi:

Enlightenment – a trilogy
for young adults:
A young teenager discovers secrets
about his heritage and is thrown
into a dangerous and challenging
position on not only his own earth
but also on another planet in…

Enlightenment: This Earth
Enlightenment: Another Earth
Enlightenment: Colliding Earths

The Equals – In a world where
humans are not the only race,
who polices the vampires?

Crime:

The Figure – The prequel to Revenge,
a gripping crime story, guess
the mysterious assassin?

Deadvent Calander – A race against
time in the run up to Xmas. Murder
and mayhem across the world!

Psychological Mystery:

Our Lives – Where friends, sex,
lies and murder are involved,
who can you trust?

For all books by Ken Kirkberry go to:

Facebook: *ken.kirkberry.9*

Amazon: *Ken Kirkberry*

Twitter: *@KKirkberry*

Printed in Great Britain
by Amazon

22091133R00099